THE LOVE CHILD

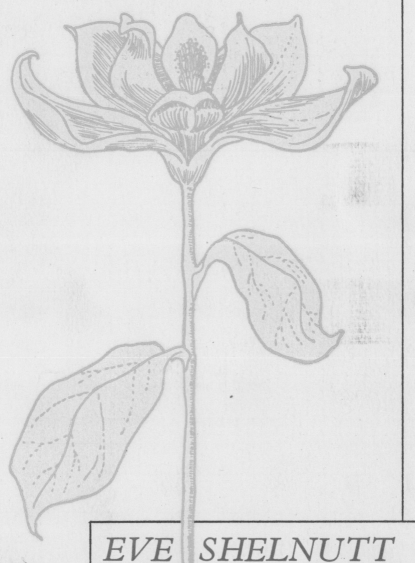

EVE SHELNUTT

EVE SHELNUTT
THE LOVE CHILD

Santa Barbara
BLACK SPARROW PRESS
1979

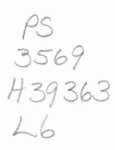

3/1979
Am Lit. Con

ACKNOWLEDGEMENT

Grateful acknowledgement is given to the editors of the following periodicals where some of these stories originally appeared: *American Review, Carolina Quarterly, Graffiti, Greensboro Review, Hawaii Review, The Literary Review, Mississippi Review, Mother Jones, Northwest Review, O. Henry Prize Stories, Ohio Review, Ploughshares, Prairie Schooner, Roanoke Review, Shenandoah, Stories of the Modern South, Virginia Quarterly Review.*

LIBRARY OF CONGRESS CATALOGING IN PUBLICATION DATA

Shelnutt, Eve, 1943-
  The love child.

  I. Title.
PZ4.S5453Lo   [PS3569.H39363]   813'.5'4   78-27484
ISBN 0-87685-384-X (paper edition)
ISBN 0-87685-385-8 (signed cloth edition)

to Fred Chappell

Semblance is wrought over all things.

—Xenophanes

TABLE OF CONTENTS

The Love Child

Grace

When Jim Kuykendall was 39 and had been a father for nine of those years, he bought a restaurant and he named it The Carousel.

It was on the old highway, *near* the new highway where there were no trees at all and where the sun was so white the thighs of the girl on the whiskey billboard protruded. She looked headless.

Drivers might tire of this new road, even of the yellow line muted as the eyes of an albino.

On the old road then he painted The Carousel bright, bright blue, which had been his favorite color for so long that he had dressed his mother in death in the bluest dress of velvet. He strung around it, too, streamers of Cadillac-gold, and he put peacock feathers in blue vases in the windows. Before the windows began steaming from hot dog vapors and the floating oils of french fries, the feathers in the window-light took on the color of the six-sided building, as if the bird himself had been artificial.

His sister Myrtle said, "Oh Jimmy, it's just *like* you," meaning the incomplete picture. To put herself in it, she squeezed Jim around the waist and later she put on a blue apron whose bib came just to her breasts, and she began wiping off tables with a rag.

Yet: he wouldn't let her cook the special dishes—bean soup, La Guardia chili ("*Hot*, get it?" Jim said, winking)—or call out the diminutive "B.L.T.'s," so when customers came, Myrtle rolled her eyes toward him in the back and took orders in a prissy voice. What does she *know?* they asked themselves.

Some came. Some, seeing the circular drive and the gold spinners, thought it was a drive-in. They parked their cars in a circle, nose or eagle or elevated custom hood almost flush with the blue building. Then, after getting over the fact that they had been wrong, they liked looking through the steam at their cars so close, as if babies slept in the back seats.

Aiken, South Carolina is flat, or the rises fit against the sky as closely as a man's hand on a woman's belly. New and like eruptions of a time that would pass, two aircraft companies came and put up buildings white as sun. The men went in like moths. Now they were richer, and they weren't sure how to spend. Their wives showed them, page by page or window by window, but everything the men saw had a dimension which seemed measurable. Some of those men stopped at The Carousel, the sight of peacock feathers ruffling involuntary muscles.

The father wouldn't let them play the juke box. He put nylon tape across the buttons, and Tammy Wynette might as well have been dead. The men themselves looked enough like Ferlin Huskey. The women who came, who were not wives and who were so young they might wonder when their own men would grow dangerous enough to resemble these men—the red noses, the high-flame cheeks against cheek-bone tans—they didn't need also Ferlin's voice to loosen the hips like their wide-vision eyes.

So Jim brought his own record player and two L.P.'s—"Never the Lonely," Frank Sinatra, and "Cry Me a River" by Julie London, his favorite.

"Come on, Jimmy, pretty-please," a girl said, just like Myrtle might. "Take the tape off, will you?"

He stopped by her table, napkin-collared tea glass in hand, and he sang to her:

"Now you say you love me.
Well, just to prove you do,
Come on and cry me a river,
Cry me a river.
I cried a river over you."

"I'll never eat anywhere else as long as I live," she said.

Coy, Myrtle's husband, begrudged Jim the tiny room in their apartment, one next to the bathroom and with a high window, airless. Whenever he ate or watched ball games on T.V., Coy said, "In the Navy, by God, we . . . ." And even a stranger walking in could have known that *Jim* had never been in the Navy, which was one reason Myrtle sat on his bed Sunday afternoons, filing her nails and listening to Frank Sinatra on his second-best player. Coy felt outnumbered, a real estate man in a sold-out county.

"Do you think," Myrtle asked, looking on his dresser at their mother's photograph, "she suffered?"

"Sure," said Jim, and she shivered while he watched her.

Before the winter drizzles began, the father discovered the fishing places in Aiken. He had the colored boy come in from out back and cook, and for the duration, he let Rufus wear one of his houndstooth suit-coats. Evenings, around five when, if this had been farm country, the sound of small bells and the smell of food would be mingling, Jim came into The Carousel with fresh fish and he cooked it up for whoever was there. Not on the menu, a variable price. "Damn-ass chiggers, no sweet local talent with me to throw in a line. . . . That'll be $2.75," he said. And the way he laughed told the men who wanted to learn how to spend that this was it.

Then the rains started. Some of the girls skipped school altogether and sat in two's and three's with their cigarettes burning close enough to the windows to make tiny holes in the vapors from which to watch the cars go past. And with most of the men at work, they had Jim to themselves. He sat on a stool by the cash register and made notations on an old receipt.

"What are you doing way over there?" they asked, and he said it was nothing they should worry their pretty little heads about, and so they didn't—fish sleepy in deep waters.

The men punched out early on a grievance against the weather, and they came and ate some of Myrtle's Eagle Brand condensed milk lemon pie and drank coffee and were late for their substantial meals.

No one new stopped in, The Carousel in a haze and the coated windows like a refraction. Except Coy, who had never been in and who, on seeing Myrtle there the one night, said, "Get yourself home and get a *bra* on." Coy let water drip from his raincoat onto the piece of carpet by the cigarette machine, and while he wiped his head with a handkerchief he told Jim he had something for him—two cartons of Nifty sugar packets, 10,000 teaspoons of sugar in all, from a train wreck which none of them inside The Carousel had heard about.

Outside, the gold spinners flapped loose around the two telephone poles on either side of the drive; Coy said the place was going to pot. Then, when Jim brought the two cases of Nifty sugar packs back to his room and Coy saw them there that first evening after the wreck, he said to Myrtle, By-God-in-the-Navy-you-didn't-look-a-gift-horse-in-the-mouth. "That's it," he said, "I mean that is *it*."

"Well, you know him," Myrtle said, and he didn't and she knew it.

But a gesture: Coy let the father have his daughter come down by bus from Rutherfordton—alone, even though she was only nine, with his features— the Philistine nose and eyes of royal blue—which made Myrtle say as she looked at the photograph, "She'll make it."

Jim forgot she was coming. It was Rufus, coming in with the garbage cans, who said, "Is the kid in-dare yet?" because he had a vision of her being dressed in midget-men's pants and french cuffs and a houndstooth jacket, as completely done as a pork roast or a half-child bottled at a fair.

Myrtle clapped her hand over her mouth and the father popped a mint in his mouth and ran, and he found her, hands folded in her lap, feet dangling, in the center of the Greyhound Bus Station. She wouldn't cry.

He took her straight to The Carousel. He looked over all the booths as he sat her at the counter and spun her around until she stopped facing them. Jim tapped his fingers on the counter and it was quiet as closet-prayer in the room. He looked up and he said, "I'll kill anybody who touches her." And the daughter, who had not yet felt the movement of the body which makes a woman go senseless in the hold of a man, felt it then, and Jim slapped the counter, waking her from the first real sleep. "So you name it, honey," he said, "and I'll cook it up pronto."

Myrtle called, "Give her a Baby Ruth and let her rest, will you!" Which almost broke the father's spell, and the girl could sit looking out, as if the men were distant as ships in a rain of whispering.

Her mother was like a bird, a hybrid-species with lesser plumage, legs of the bantam, the dove's breast, so now, the men, imagining how this girl might turn out eventually, imagined by chance a woman like the mother. And because all of them could not easily fit their bodies next to the bodies of their wives—even though this fact was still a surprise and a transgression of their belief that all human bodies could somehow fit, which made them practice in anger, hatred of the least fat or wrinkle—because they had these secrets, the men imagined suddenly that they knew why Jim was at The Carousel and not in some other place. They thought, that night, the food tasted especially good and, secretly, they were proud of him. They would not have laid one finger on that girl, death or not as a promise.

The daughter ate too much, every dish Jim brought out—fried bread and hot chilies, a sticky-bun, scrambled eggs with Dijon mustard, a bowl of grits. And when she went to the bathroom, his one spotless room with "All" on the door, it was as if her insides would come out. Then she fell asleep on the commode. Myrtle brought her out; Jim said *she* ought to, and while he stacked the receipts and the last few men counted their change, the girl sat sleeping on the old Hudson car seat in the foyer by the door. A single cricket rubbed his legs together on the tile floor and it was not at all like a fieldful. A man with one hand on the door and the other fingering pocket change looked down at her white knee socks bunched at her ankles. Looking from her to the father, his neck lowered in his collar and his head wobbled snake-like as if he were trying to sense a danger.

Coy looked up from the late-night news as they brought her in, and he had nothing to say, even when Myrtle waited by him on the couch, heavy like a pillow embroidered with a verse from The Gospels.

"Shit, shit, shit," the father said to himself in the bedroom—softly, and it carried because the particular news reporter was a frantic man with vacant spaces in his voice register. Coy and Myrtle pretended not to hear.

She woke on the pallet on the floor and looked at his room—the stack of maroon, monogrammed towels folded in a pillow-shape. And on top of a box, a smaller box filled with gold, silver, and blue cuff links. A bar of soap with the imprint of a ship hung from a rope on the door knob and up higher six identical starched blue shirts hung on a nail.

And him: he slept in nylon pajamas the color of the towels, wild berries, or church satin and Christ's blood when it is served in tiny glasses.

That morning she didn't eat. When Jim drove her to The Carousel, he turned to her when they were still on the highway and said, "Look at that, will you look at that," and she turned all the way around in her seat trying to see a wreck or a possum dead on the road.

He meant the signs. In the night a customer had ringed The Carousel with signs which said "Eat" on one and "Here" on another, and "Best" on one and "Food" on another, and "Real" on one and "Service" on another.

"Jesus Christ," her father said as he pulled them up and broke them and stuffed them in Rufus' garbage cans. She watched.

Myrtle came flying into the drive in Coy's company car on which he had lettered, "Buy from a shrewd man," and Myrtle screamed at Jim, "How'd I know you had her! I've been all over that complex looking in the swings, for Pete's sake."

"She's mine," he said, "so I'd have her, honey."

They opened up and all day he would not let her try to cook or lay silver or fill the shakers with salt. She sat where he put her, next to the three-tiered pie keeper, and when she turned to look out, her pigtails brushed on the plastic.

"Gotcha a girl, huh?" the women said. The men studied her. If she had an arm resting on the counter, they might stop and put one of their arms near hers and turn to say to anybody, "She's white, she's so white."

"Why don't you make a whole *batch* of tea up, like Momma does?" she would ask Jim.

"*Sours* it," he would say.

"Where are the rest of the people?" she would ask.

"In love," he would say.

Then that night she slept and the next day was the last day, and Myrtle begged Jim to let her and the girl stay home so Myrtle could introduce her around and let her go into their apartments and see all the pretty things.

"*No.*"

"I could take her around and show her all kinds of things Momma had. She never got to see Momma's things, remember," Myrtle whined, and Jim said, "You do it then, you do it."

An organ in miniature, a white glass rooster with pins inside its belly, a *Sacred Heart Reader*, a 24-inch T.V., beaded satin slippers, teeth in a jar, red milk glass the color of Jim's pajamas, and, most of all, a see-through picture of Christ kneeling in Gethsemane, a light bulb above His head where God would be.

Then Jim called home at noon and Myrtle brought the daughter to The Carousel, and he fixed her his special dinner—laid on a white cloth, milk in a stemmed glass which he said she could take home, and some of his half of the sterling silver from the girl's mother's house, a plate with gold rimming, and a tiny swan with salt between its wings. She sat by herself and he waited on her, looking down over her shoulder. "Like it, honey?" he said.

Rufus came to stand behind the grill to watch.

And the men watched, and the women, walking by Jim, squeezed his arm and did not pop their gum. Hardly anyone came for supper. Jim closed early and drove her himself to the bus station.

Myrtle drove up just as the bus was pulling out—in Coy's second car, Coy on the passenger side. Myrtle waved and waved. Jim put his fingers to his lips and blew the daughter a kiss, and then the girl waved back, the stemmed glass he had given her in the waving hand, partially wrapped, catching light.

Jim said to Myrtle, "Well."

During the wet season, one of the two aircraft companies went out of business, as if a whole succession of doves had been sent out and returned leafless. For a short time, the regulars at The Carousel were giddy with time and severance pay. Then Rufus became especially solemn.

One night when it was moonless and cold, the daughter woke to find herself in the mother's car. She looked over the front seat and saw a map spread on the seat by her mother, who smoked and dimmed the lights in a rhythm even though no cars were coming. In the car's hum, she slept again, knowing where they were headed, the knowledge a room in which she wouldn't cry.

On the old road the father was waving, flagging down their Nash Ambassador, everything dark but the headlights on him and on the refrigerator of stainless steel beside him, monument-tall.

"Hi, honey," Jim said to the girl, patting her head through the window. Then to the mother: "They repossess tomorrow, so this is it. Back her around," he said, meaning the tiny trailer attached to the Nash. For this the mother threw her cigarette out the window and concentrated.

The girl jumped out and stood watching them push the refrigerator up two boards onto the trailer, his voice the one she listened to, saying, "Easy, easy," and "Shit, no," and "O.K." Light fringed the sky, finally, and he came to where she stood, by The Carousel door, and he patted her head and carried her back to the car. "See you before you know it," he said, and he shut the door behind her and waved as the mother turned in the direction in which they had come.

Then he drove off; the girl saw that.

At home, the refrigerator seemed to take up all of the four rooms. And often, when she was roller skating alone, the girl thought that if it were left outside, *two* children could climb in to hide, one in each door, and after the screaming seemed useless, could die together, talking.

It was a long time before the father saw the daughter again. On a birthday, he sent her a Hurlburt's Children's Bible, red, with her name pressed in gold letters in its lower right-hand corner. Inside on his business card he had written, "My love to my love," and the card itself said, "Buy a Bible from a good man." Inside the book were pictures in color and they were beautiful.

When the daughter was sixteen, he wrote her a post card and said she should get on a bus and come to Jacksonville, Florida for a vacation, and that he would be there on August 12th in the Greyhound Bus Station, so she went.

It was her first vacation. After showing her his room, on the outskirts of Jacksonville in a concrete house where a man with tanned cheeks and arms lived with a fat wife and so many children that the father had to keep his things folded in his room—after that, he took her to the ocean, to a motel suite with a kitchen, sitting room, and bedroom. And for a week he cooked for her. He taught her how to play shuffleboard and how to jump waves. She tanned and he said that *she* was beautiful. At the bus station, he gave her a necklace with one tiny pearl on a silver chain. "Be good," he called to her, and, through the window, he looked to her the same.

In time, the daughter became the kind of woman who owns few things. She became the kind of woman whose eyes talk. She didn't think about owning a man in marriage—his Hot Point range and children who might look like him. And of the men she had, she didn't ask if they were married, or had been, or wanted to be. In this way she became the kind of woman who frightens some men. Watching her walk loose-hipped, they had to decide—*if* she looked at them and if she decided: "Yes," eyeing the one body—whether or not they wanted to hear a sound not quite human when she broke and became herself under them. About which there was nothing to say: How she became this sort of woman who does not belong.

The father, however, in a room, in sleep, grinding his teeth when the mouth tastes salt and dreams come in waves: In sleep he knew: If a light shone on this daughter from high up, she would in those rocking beds shine, one looping dip after another, along her whole body: light, and knew that she would appear armless like the first fish in first-water time when air and salt met.

The Apprentice

She leaves him in a well-ordered room, with even the wilted daisies drawn from the vase of others still fresh. This order is a rule with her though she does not know there is a strictness about this other life beginning. Like a new baby, she is on a schedule. Someone feeds her; she thinks it is her husband. He is a good man. On schedule, she stands at the doorway, on her way out for a package of cigarettes, and, looking at him bent over his papers, she thinks: "He is a good man. I married a good man." He has the kind of face which looks healthy in any light. She has refused for months to go into K-Mart with him to buy tools and car oil. She says the fluorescent lighting makes everyone appear deadskinned. But not him. Sometimes she is able to see him at the checkout counter from where she waits in the car. At those times she imagines that his skin is growing even more healthy under the glare which is like that glare the police use to wear their suspects down into confession. He is so good he will last forever.

Now, at the door, she says twice to herself, "Good, good," and this is part of the schedule. It is a self-adjusting schedule; it speeds up of its own accord. Years ago Anne would never have considered making words of her feelings for him. Before the year is out, she will be able to talk about him in whole sentences. It is what feels like cause and effect that she is learning: how things work. A baby, once having discovered his mouth, uses it; it fills up—food, liquid, words. The mother would cry if the baby did not use his mouth. If he did not use his mouth, the doctors would attach wires and pieces of plastic to the skin, in and out. It would be a mess, an unholy thing.

21

"I'm going out for cigarettes," she says to him, "to Kroger's. I'll be right back."

He does not ask why she is always out of Winstons at eight-thirty at night. He may notice that the porch light behind her head makes her brown hair appear golden, that the sound of crickets in the bushes is like perfume, that she has become prettier: if there had been babies, she might appear weighted down, like a pear tree in season. As it may be to him, she is like a reed on which her hair blows. Her dress is wheat-colored, the color of the rug, the same color as sand on a Texas farm. It was a long time ago that he originated from any place, but it may have been a Texas farm. All the colors in their house are made from that sandy base color, as if they had added varying amounts of red clay, from another section of the country, to each fabric and texture. If either of them wore pure red, he would be surprised; his eyes would jump. She should give up smoking. He has, in fact, never seen her smoke. But he doesn't think of this. In his hands is a sheath of papers filled with numbers which mean production is up or down or maintaining its own equilibrium. What is it his company makes? She asks him that sometimes, then she forgets his answer. And so she leaves him with his head bent over the table. It could be years ago; he could be an accountant in another country. It is an old, old profession. She married him because he did not do something newfangled.

But, of course, she has not *always* gone out at eight-thirty at night, and he was not always an accountant. But who, on an investigation of the neighborbood, would know? The maids who have finished serving dinner to their employers are lined up along the street, their dresses like muted lights which children need in their rooms if their dreams are of warlocks or horses—blue, yellow, occasionally crimson. They are waiting for men who come in cars blue, yellow, or crimson. Very little food is actually blue; it is against some natural law. She could herself get into one of those cars with big tires. She could go over to the East End tonight; there are possibilities. But she does not think of them in that way because she is busy in another motion, taking short steps. She is too tall, she feels hindered.

The cat woman is oh so much shorter. When Anne sees her this time, her own limbs feel overgrown, as if she were of the wrong species. This sensation is not unlike that which a woman feels when, after having imagined a particular man, she finds herself next to him, fitting into the vacant spaces where all left out feels exposed, as if in danger.

It is almost the end of twilight, when the sky is the color of the old woman's shopping bag. The cat woman is finding flowers; she is like a lichee nut. The sweet inside pulp smells of carnations, and they are in sight, sticking from a garbage can beside the florist's shop. But this is not a matter for the brain; the nose is a double lens from which the sweet pulp sees. They are every odor, but not brown. Anne does not smoke. It would be harmful to her lungs. This older woman is preserved like candied ginger lying in her own box. She will be given to the mortuary, and they don't like ginger. The flowers are almost new, anyone would calculate twenty-four hours old, not old in some relation. The cat woman knows this. Anne sees she is no fool; some breathing is like a flower almost dead, a flower unworthy of a sick person or of a mother. Some breathing begins as if all air were old, used air, as in artificial respiration when mouth to mouth is the best available; and then it seems that air will burst, like a country girl shown a good man.

The cat woman knows how to lift garbage cans as if the cans had rubber lids, lip-soft. She pulls out also an electric cord, the kind left exposed and hanging down, in movies about the Gestapo, even when the year 1942 isn't mentioned. It is the kind of cord which sometimes drops from the ceiling into bath tubs, and Peter Lorre does not look at the floating body with burned hair like shriveled nerves. He looks up at the ceiling and shakes his eyes. Anne knows fifty uses for this electric cord now. The cat woman is sharp; she would not paint her toe nails in the bath tub as Anne did once a week, until now. There is a crust of dirt on the old woman's shoes, thick as cats' paws. Anne wants to hear her talk. What sound?

The families in which all the members are deaf often choose not to make those sounds which are imitations of no one they love. Their hands become like leaves in the wind of a spongy brain when an idea steps it flat; wounds of hands, like ballet when the women are all virgins. But the cat woman has been under someone; Anne can see, as if the impression of teeth were still visible. Take a rabbit from the mouth of a snake, what her husband would know if he came from Texas. Cook it, even in wine, and the teeth marks are in the belly. On eating, they taste like salt, and, even if frozen, years later the taste of salt is still embedded in the flesh. Her color is puce; her legs have parted.

Anne buys herself a shopping bag with handles in the grocery store. There two men walk the aisles—one of them is a doll, the other is a string bag which holds the doll and the cart and the food. The doll's baby fat has returned to the belly, but the string bag is taut and weighted down. He has done lifting, so it is to Anne funny who pushes the cart and who follows. They are prettier than she. If one threw the other out, nothing would come of either of them, no new thing like this she sees, the inseparable men married to a motion all their own—a new species. Because there are things she has not noticed before, she thinks: and why not? if they learned how to fit after numberless adjustments. The doll's toes probably ached for months, he is so short and was not young enough for the new shoes they manufacture now to make feet stronger even in the toes. Coming out with her bag, she sees them get from their Porsche their two dogs which do not go together so that they make their owners dance in self-made choreography around them. But the cat woman knew better, and when Anne goes to the corner where she can watch the bedding down of the cats and the woman, it is that her shoulders let loose, the grace of motion in the cats and the woman a massage. When the cats cry, Anne thinks it is herself.

The moonlight is honey. The old woman builds her pallet of cat fur and her own padding—why she is squat and on her fanny another padding deep as paw—against a fence, a comb to which the honey sticks. The shopkeepers probably know the woman with her cats sleeps here, but she is not sweet *outside*; she has a shell, and if Anne would hear her talk, she must make short steps and fold her body shorter, and carry her brown bag as if it held something—her husband's papers, that weight, so she imagines numbers on white pages until her arms sag. And why does he hold them to the light, until the paper itself is translucent, how a face can be when the man wants to see, and will touch her until she is inside a candle? If he has lit his own face with her, she has forgotten. Her mouth tastes salt, and maybe when the old woman holds the largest cat against her belly, he tastes it too, because she has been bitten once. The old woman's fingers move across the fur, and then the cat bites. The scream is how bees must sound when the honey goes into a pail. Anne hears a sound which her husband makes with his tongue when he is sleeping with one hand on her and another on himself. Then, even if she has been sleeping, she wakes and lies near his mouth, as if the sound could divine words. He could tell her what country he came from, what origin he had said before she forgot.

She walks up to the woman bent over her wound, and she says as if to a child, "Let me see." Like a child, the old woman holds her loose skin up. To Anne it is exposed in the way a patient's area of skin is open in the surrounding sterile cotton. The surgeons try to concentrate; it pays not to think of the patient's history, who might cry when the mortuary gets the box of ginger, and the mouth is bitter.

"I've seen you," the cat woman says.

"I've seen you too," Anne answers. If they were both children, they would share a string bag and the rag doll inside. The skin Anne holds up is ridged like twine. "It's not bad," she says. "Do you sleep here all the time?" The fluorescent lights go off in the store to which the woman's fence is attached. Anne wants to smoke a cigarette and see the smoke catch the moonlight, as if she could talk if her fingers held smoke.

"I used not to," the old woman answers, "but I do. They wanted more rent. Then I moved and I couldn't take the cats. I love the cats. I have lots of cats, like babies."

To Anne they are not like babies; she wants to explain how not, to set her straight, if she knew hand language, to tell her how her husband made motions on her stomach, asking if she wanted a baby, as if his fingers dipping down into her skin would bring one out; yet, at the times when he lifted his empty hands up above the sheet for her to see that they were empty, she would be glad that in fact his fingers held nothing, because in the light she would imagine shapes not human. How the woman held the cat, and why the cat had bitten her.

Her husband would wonder where she was. He might look out the door and imagine her running on the rail fence by their driveway, stoop and call, make clicking noises with his tongue. So she could not go back right away, because he might pick her up by the neck and place her near his neck where it was warm, because he was not only good, but capable of *extensions:* she had seen him go from one place to another, from where he started to where he was. She could now give recitations, if anyone asked, as if she had just remembered places. It would be nice to tell someone now, before she forgot. To be sociable, she sits beside the cat woman, where it is warm, and asks her what she has been doing all this time. The cats play among the garbage cans. The sound is like tin tea sets on a metal table under a tree when the girls are five and the parents are sleeping in the house.

She scratches the polish off her nails while she listens, and she feels herself close in—she will be shorter when she gets home. And the dampness makes her hair come loose so that it hangs on her dress like a rag and sops the moonlight up. She is a different color.

Of course the old woman's story is something like she has imagined after watching her for weeks, because the man who married her, who had split her belly and put a baby there, who had breathed his old air into her mouth and made her mend until the belly swelled and broke—he went crazy, in the country. Everywhere there was sand, the color of the beach if you remember being taken there, and if you remember that the color is hot and it is easy to think of the color and the heat as one, until it seems you will suffocate. Her husband began sitting in the barn and looking out, perched high like a hawk, in the shade of the eaves of the barn. If it rained, he laughed, and he would draw a finger up to where the sun was being held by clouds, and he would make a sound like a machine gun. Nothing grew but the baby he pulled out of her, and that baby grew until he was big enough to set in the yard like a rooster. The husband made the boy cackle for him sometimes, after he dug the boy a tiny hole big enough for his bottom. One day the husband got the boy to cackle long enough for him to climb up to the loft of the barn, and then he took his finger out. He attached his finger to a metal piece, and then, rat tat, he shot the boy, and the boy fell over like a rooster. The husband flew down from the barn, and the cat woman said it made her sick, going out to pick them up. She told Anne that if she had a baby, she better get more than one, how men were, making stories come out like that. Cats multiply fast.

But Anne is sick already, as if her stomach were swollen and it were already morning when women pull themselves out of covers to hang their mouths over commodes and retch, because the baby doesn't like putridness inside its home. When she gets up, the cat woman is asleep, and her mouth appears hammered shut by tiny nails. There were experiments with nails during the war, and when the people came out, they moved differently, but enough of them moved the same that they told a lie. They allowed the watchers to imagine each story was something alike, and it could be this old woman lied. It could be Anne is not good at reading motion that goes with words. Then, it appears that the old woman's skin, while Anne turns to look backwards, is growing more healthy, and only Anne is brownish-purple.

When she is home and her shopping bag stuffed beside the refrigerator where all the grocery bags are stored, she goes over to him and lifts his head up, and he wakes up, but she has timing he can't have, just having awakened. She raises a finger to her lips and she smiles, she smiles the way he likes from another time he can't remember in preciseness while he is just waking. But Anne puts his fingers on his face, then she puts one finger on her thigh. She does not let him press his finger on her skin until she leads him to another room. There it is darker, the light from the street lamp comes through the blinds at points, scattered light, in particles. She takes a finger and puts it on a leg. When he presses down, what he remembers shows in his face as surprise. Her skin hardly gives, it is tight, as if she were very, very young. He looks at her in amazement because it does not feel that his hands would go in and bring nothing out.

So he does not hold his hands up empty in the light for her to see. He burrows himself in her, finally, with a sound, leaving something in her so that, for the first time since she can remember, he is not lazy and slow. He looks at her as if he were in sunlight, and he can't recall that the heat often becomes too hot. He forgets to calculate, and Anne looks up at him as if she were counting.

She begins to wait, on schedule. Before she sleeps, there are shapes to notice: the cat woman turns in her sleep exactly as Anne's husband turns. Anne, herself, moves as if fitting with a particular man she has imagined for years. Something which can be seen from high up, as a hawk sees, is exposed.

The night feels like a boat inside which these people are dreaming. It may rain for forty nights while they multiply in kind.

Angel

It is a long ride up the mountain. The car is too small, as any car would be, because the mother and the cousin are larger than usual women. It is not *grotesque* cargo. Simply: these two women are oversized enough to be burdensome in a way not easily dismissed, as when a person sniffs an odor he can't place, and suddenly the nose is all the face remembers of itself.

Then, there's the daughter, in the back with a dress-box.

Inside the box is a dress, almost like another person—compact.

Lois, the mother, and Helen, the cousin, have been fussing over the dress for weeks. The second daughter, the person who is related because they know where to find her, and how her handwriting is, and what color her favorite underwear, is supposed to wear the dress for her recital in the afternoon. If they don't get the chiffon dress to the little college room in time, she will have to wear a borrowed dress. Then, she would be less related. Already she is distant. Her distance is why they hurry to her. They must get the dress, which they have, on her whom they haven't.

Of the daughter inside the car—she has thought too much. They don't like her because she thinks. She should hibernate; they need time off. As it is, they keep their eyes on the curves ahead, like beasts taking courage from the feel of muscles inside.

She: she imagines the father they won't speak of is on the car carrier, windfilled. Up there, what does he think of her, quick! before dust fills his mouth. *"Never mind,"* he answers. So she settles for the possible: he wouldn't miss the recital. He, in some way, claims this other daughter more

29

than they. He and she are lost together. Claire, her name is, a bell-sound. Yet, this trio in the car will suit him up when he dies and someone calls (for he has *their* address, not the other way around). Still, they might not know his size; they might have to wire his sister and ask.

And on the chiffon dress, it is the hem which they can't get straight. *His* are the owl-eyes. The whole head moves to a sight. He never over-ate.

Half-way, they stop at an Inn where fish oil is in the air, in the threads of the gingham curtains, in the fibers of the floor, and on the chrome napkin holder. They order fish.

"Amaze me," the daughter says, and she sits opposite to watch.

Really, they have ceased to look at one another when she says something, and this cessation makes her both more distant and more close, or a combination of the two, as in films when the long shot fades to the close-up shot.

Now she sees the down on the cousin's face. Helen is next to the window; sunlight is coming over her left shoulder and onto her left cheek where a thousand tiny hairs cover the acne scars. The same down is on her lip-line and on her arms and, presumbably, between her thighs. A soft yellow fur. She looks broader than she is, and nowhere does her dress stick flat on her skin, as if the fur held up the cloth. To go with this yellow, she wears oranges and browns. She puts ketchup on her fish, and her large fingers turn the hush puppies into the red on the plate.

"Pass the salt," they say to each other. They are very much at home here. This is where they stop on each trip to the other daughter, and now the owner of the Inn knows where they are headed.

The mother chews with one hand near her mouth. There are defects on all their bodies. But none of these defects is physical so much as rhythmical— the mother's hand is *arrested* at the mouth when the mouth chews, because once the mother had embarrassing tooth-trouble, and the palm which sought to hush the cracking sound the jaw made (a hollow nothing-crack with the open and shut) failed. And now the mouth condemns the hand by making it stay where it shouldn't when the rest of the body has moved on. And because the father left Lois, her stomach feels too large. She is continuously pressing down on it. When she stands, she feels her ribcage first, as if to locate the last, and missing, rib.

And they are fat, not very fat, but when they sit, their legs sprawl from the weight, and they are always trying to find a place to lie down for rests. Their feet are skinny, more like hands. They like to eat, since, afterwards, the smoking tastes better, and when they smoke, it is the longest part of the meal, with coffee, until the taste of grease is gone, and the taste of smoke is more like it was when they began to smoke. When they smoke in the car, they first take out the thermos of coffee and pour themselves amounts almost measured, and then they light up. Now they pass each other a last shared cigarette. Its filter has two colors of lipstick because this cigarette is the final thing to do in the Inn, after the trip to the bathroom and the stretching behind the chairs to pull the muscles long before bending them short inside the car again.

"Oh my God," Lois says. "Look at the time."

Pauline *knows* this isn't their lives. *She* is small, and when she is younger and first beginning to notice how the body can tell on a person, she imagines her very smallness will save her. She stands on the top of her dressing table, turns backwards, and looks at her face from between the backs of her knees, just to see how a face like hers might look upside down and backwards. She imagines, then, nothing will surprise her, not even the tiny mole such as the father grew after thirty-five years, on his left side and just above the pajama-line, a mole minty-brown and white-flecked.

And there is less of herself to police, not more than five feet and three and one-quarter inches. When Helen and Lois turn to look back at the possum dead on the road, so newly dead his blood marks the tires and the tires mark the road, they hardly see her, in the middle, between the backs of Helen, who never drives, and Lois, who drives. Too, she is quiet, like a string. Nothing moves inside her she doesn't know about. She would leave her address with anyone, her size sewn in any coat, her letters tied in blue ribbons, and everything she has owned laid out on the bed, on the white coverlet, as in wedding rituals and deaths.

What she thinks of the father: is that *when* he dies, it will be like a setting of sterling, burnt mellow with polish, light and dark, the head like a soup spoon laid across the upper part of a butter dish. Then she will come, a promise. And pull all the pieces into a bundle, and wrap it in navy-blue velvet, and put it very carefully back into the mahogany box. The rest of them will laugh, as at a great party where no one knows how to behave when the formal setting is laid.

"What if a tire blows?" the mother asks the cousin.

"I would hitch-hike," the cousin answers.

"You!" the mother laughs. "Light me up one."

When Helen moves, it is slowly, always. She's had three children, who surprise her. She doesn't like to stay home with them. She comes by bus to Lois's house where the child is not really a child and where the piano takes up so much of the living room she fits in with her slow movements. She has yet to break an ashtray. In a way, she is trying to catch up with her children—she pores over the picture album of Lois and Lois's two girls, and the father— pictured in every kind of light with one hand on the car door and one hand at his necktie. In the album, Lois is last seen holding the girls when the girls are waist-high to Lois, and then, the girls begin to hate the camera; they look at it as if it were a man spying.

Pauline, herself, takes the album out secretly, and on Sundays, when Helen and Lois are in church, she shades the pictures with a lead pencil, very lightly but over and over, at intervals. She leaves his face bright, because she forgets, almost, how it was.

How it was when he brought gifts: he *smiled*, into the money (I was sixteen myself, he says, before *I* got the goods), and the money showing so that he begins to miss certain other sights around the house that Pauline doesn't miss.

"What I thought of you then . . ." is how she wants to begin now, at this age, maybe over coffee at Howard Johnsons, since he thinks of Howard Johnsons as the place to eat, and she hasn't been able to tell him otherwise, about the color aqua.

He comes in without knocking, barely able to see over the presents, with little, important boxes from jewelry shops sticking from his pockets. "Never mind your hair," he says to Lois. "*Look*." He doesn't see the cracks in her lips, or the gray right behind the face-skin, or the fat unless he pinches her fanny.

He thinks the pale-blue satin gown from Atlanta or New York, with its rhinestone trim from neck to floor, and its fringed sash, looks *fine*.

Lois, of course, puts on the satin robe, and sometime later, when he can't be found, as if he had forgotten his manners, she puts the robe on again, to hang herself in, up high on the chandelier, and Pauline knows it will be something like this to tell him about the robe. It is a *picture*: the neck is swollen, and the hand tucks just inside the rope for breathing space, and it is swollen, and the ankles sticking out from the satin robe are swollen. And the voice is froggish. "*Well*, HELP!"

He doesn't notice, either, how they smell—from what they eat and don't get to eat. He brings the present of a crate of oranges, a crate of grapefruit, tins of liver pâté, and boxes of crackers, and cans of oysters, and cans of ham, and a brown mustard, and many kinds of cheese, and sometimes wine, and they eat on the floor, around the presents and his suitcase where something forgotten, some littler present, might be found; and truly, he doesn't notice.

Lois stops the car so fast, it's as if a tire *has* blown, and they are off the pavement into the gravel before Pauline sees the apple stand. But Helen has seen it, maybe miles ahead, or smelled it, and she's got change jingling. She hops out, fast for her, and says, "Peck, red ones," and "Here," and then they eat, three each until the two mouths must taste acid, and the two stomachs must churn. In the car is the smell of apple juice, fine little sprays which catch some light, and fall, and the smell of smoke caught in sunlight, and their Prince Charles perfume, cologne, or powder.

Claire's room, in past-time, smells of the big blue box, on her side of the room, by the bed and under the window, and with no electricity when the bill's not paid, if Pauline wants to see what's new in the box, she sees it in this window-light—pictures from magazines: ladies, lovely ladies with fine hair like Claire's when it is clean, and long fingernails, and pink toes, and, sometimes, men standing behind these ladies, darker, with sunglasses in their hands, or wine glasses, or flowers. Or clippings about how to make a curl, or how to pull out the hair over the lip or the eyes. Or drawings of stomachs in which parts of babies are penciled in lighter colors, looking like tadpoles, some with tails and some without. And lists, in Claire's fancy writing:

> "Be kind.
> Be kind regardless.
> Smile at least once a day, to help face muscles.
> Read less; think more.
> Imagine FUTURE.
> Gain five pounds in the legs.
> Learn to play the piano."

In the bottom of the box are two dried apples, studded with cloves and decorated with blue ribbon. And old candy-wrappers, and bobby pins and lipsticks, a box of Brazil nuts, unopened.

They don't talk, Claire and Pauline. Pauline, in the past, is afraid to talk to her, and Claire doesn't talk to anyone. But Claire leaves the top of the box open. It is the only mystery in the house, and the house is so small there is nowhere to be on days when it rains but in the room with the box, and nowhere to be when Claire is taking wash-ups but in the room, alone with the box.

"She *lies*," Lois says. "You know she lies—he isn't *fat*, no fatter than me, and you know I wouldn't marry a fat man, not after *him*, Oh God, he was a sexy man. He ruined me, you know that?"

Helen chews on a red nail; she nods.

And it's true: Pauline lies, telling her version when she knows it isn't anything like theirs, feisty Pauline, who gets Claire the piano by forging Claire's handwriting, and making up a new sixteenth-birthday list with "PIANO" first, and second, and third, when Claire can't even imagine a real live piano. But then, when it's crowded out two stuffed chairs and the bookcaseful of encyclopedias Lois traded for the second-hand piano, and Claire practices what she knew already and the tiny, tiny lessons just made her remember, Lois says, "Look! She has got the longest, the absolute longest fingers. And yellow hair, I swear it's yellow, and she's so skinny! What's that you're playing, dear?"

"I don't know, I don't know."

"God," says Helen, "The hair, I mean she *looks* different."

It will happen, in future-time, that Claire and Pauline will go shopping together, when Claire has gotten married and had two beautiful children, one of each kind to make it explicit, and because Claire likes to, they will go into the ugly stores with bright lights and look at material and patterns and pots and pans, together, only, for a long time, Pauline won't like what Claire picks up to look at; she won't like that it's cheap stuff. Claire won't buy, Pauline right next to her elbow, looking on like a cat.

Lois and Helen will almost cry, saying "How *could* she! She had what must have been the best figure God put on any one girl, and look! Fat, fat, the arms, even!" They will say, "Look how she moves, like she doesn't know she's fat, not that fat yet, but how *could* she is what I want to know."

And Pauline will first get more and more sleepy-looking in the face, the figure curved in and out, the eyes the only part absolutely awake, and she first believes one side of her face is growing bigger than the other side, because: of how things are.

One time at a big party, a man will look at her, studying, and later, at night, when the houseguests are supposed to be asleep, this man will knock on her door, and when she goes to see who it is, he will have on a raincoat, and he will say, "Come on, I have something to tell you," and, half-asleep, Pauline will follow him outside, in a drizzle, holding her nightgown close, and shivering, and when they are far from the house, this man will throw her on the ground and put his hands on her breasts, and when she is looking up at him, this time with eyes which seem stopped, he will take off his raincoat and show her he is naked and means to go into her, otherwise why is he so big?

What she will know is he was almost right, because, after she screams and runs, she knows he was just a little off, no words, no introduction to himself, or to her but what he got looking at her feline-like and tense, both. So Pauline's shoulders will start to let loose, and the neck will move more easily, and she will begin to imagine herself keeping a box which if filled with how-to-do clippings.

And she will notice Claire isn't fat like Helen and Lois—it is a bouncy fatness; she sings a lot and still plays, to the children. So they will go shopping, and this time, when Claire says, "You know how little money he gives me, don't you think these would look nice on the stove?" Pauline will say they really would. They will become almost sister-like, and when they put the mother away, they will divide what was in the house evenly, and not once mention that they hate all the odds and ends. In fact, they won't say anything at all that is a lie or a truth. And Pauline will read *Dr. Zhivago* twice, trying to see why it is Claire's favorite book.

And in the future, when the recital is over, Helen and Lois will come back and lie on the sectional sofa with their legs up, and smoke, and their feet will be almost touching, their heads at opposite ends of the sofa so they can look at each other while they talk, and they will say, "My God, I am so tired, these things just wear you out."

But what do *they* know? is what Pauline asks.

Then, they get to the little college town and go right to the dormitory, and up to the third floor, and into the room, and hug Claire two or three times, squashing her, and look around the room and see the bedspread with the lilac-colored leaves and fuchia flowers is still on the single bed, and the roommate they never liked who has one hand, a stub so that it seems just curved under so they think of her as sneaky, they will notice she is still the roommate, and that the other girl they don't like with the short haircut and jeans is still popping her head in the room, this time to see how Claire is coming right before her concert.

"I have simply got to lie down," Lois says, from the bed where she is watching Claire take out the dress. "I am *bushed.*"

There is the last of the sunlight in the room, on Claire's hair and making her cotton panties and bra look especially white.

"Will you look at that figure, will you?" says the girl with the short haircut, from the doorway.

"Yeah," answers Helen, "let her get dressed."

Pauline now wants something to eat, before the music, but there isn't time. She bites her lip and helps lift the dress over, and pulls the long hair out of the neckline. She tries to keep the long skirt moving, flowing, instead of hanging down straight.

"It's pretty, Momma," says Claire. "I like it, I really do, and thank you." And, before the mirror, she fluffs out her hair, and smiles at herself: a picture. She leans over to Pauline and asks, "Isn't the hem crooked? Why couldn't they get it straight?"—not meanly, curious.

"I don't know," Pauline whispers back, "the material, the material sags after it's made, I don't know for sure. I'm sorry, but don't say."

"No." She turns, she twirls out of the room, and they all clap and laugh, and Claire keeps turning until she is dizzy, and laughs, and then they have to hurry her over, across the street and into a building, and they leave her rubbing her fingers, a frightened look on her face, the head nodding as they call, Lois and Helen together, "Do good, Sugar."

Helen and Lois will get up together, in the middle of a piece by Chopin, and go out for a cigarette.

But now, in present-time, Claire walks in, not slowly—gracefully, with her shoulders back, and her head up but not looking out at the people seated below, the lights shining on the dress which she swishes with her hands so that it is never still. Then she sits and turns to the audience and smiles quickly, but Pauline sees the eyes don't really see; they are remembering, and then the fingers begin to flex. It gets very quiet, and Claire bows her head, and she plays: beautiful, and beautifully.

In the Absence of Strangers

I saw a man I knew once in the Melody Restaurant today. I go in there about once every two weeks, for their vegetables. You get two with any dinner, and they're fresh, so it's worth the one sixty-five, plus tip.

I wanted to ask him if he came in for the vegetables too, but I didn't remember in time. I eat there and always wonder why the others come. It's spacious the way cheap restaurants are, and the waitresses are seventeen-year-old girls who look happy. They try to please. The salt and pepper shakers don't match, and, often as not, the waitress will say of at least one of the three eating utensils she brings, "I better get another one—this isn't too clean." One time my neighbor came with me to eat but left instead because of a fork. Later she thought to discuss with me the superior attributes of dishwashing by automation, but I don't worry about the degree of heat necessary for cleanliness. I merely wonder if the waitress ever lets that thought pass through *her* mind.

I was surprised, then, on this particular evening, not to have that question on my mind. In the next booth was a face I knew I should remember from somewhere. We looked at each other in half glances, to deny interest, sharing the denial and uneasy about what to do next, so that the thought of eating became secondary but self-conscious. An intrusion, really, because I had, spontaneously, remembered *him*, but his place and my place as well remained hidden, like a body before the river. I suppose now, thinking back, I could have said, "Hey, where do I know you from?" I've done that before.

I tried smoking while I waited for the main course. The salad is brought

37

first, as if it were a good place, and you can tell no one finds it ironic to observe this better-restaurant ritual while also eating on formica-topped tables with the juke box selector hanging over the ketchup and mustard dispensers.

I ate the salad slowly, hoping to remember where I'd seen him, but nothing happened. I was grateful I had the habit of leaving the restaurant immediately after eating, probably because it isn't the place to linger over coffee, but also because I feel like an intruder; I see the same faces every time and am sure all the customers except for me are regulars. And now the man opposite me was an intruder also and probably didn't realize it.

I fumbled for the cigarette. I wear skirts with pockets because I despise handbags. When I carry one I am constantly checking the latch to see if anyone has picked it while I was waiting for a Don't Walk sign. It is much easier, therefore, to keep my change and keys, folding money and cigarettes close enough to my body to be able to feel them. I've never had a cent stolen from me although I still fear theft.

By the time I got the package of Winstons out of the pocket, one had fallen halfway out and was broken. I pulled it out and added it to the shredded napkin in the metal ashtray. I noticed my hands were shaking when I struck the match. He was watching me and probably had remembered me. I always feel unprotected when someone remembers me first. It gives them a chance to match images before you can compensate by trying to act however it was the last time they saw you. I have found people get uneasy if you behave differently very often.

When I finished the cigarette, he had finished his salad, and we were both fingering our water glasses, having nowhere to look but at each other or down. That must be why I usually eat at drive-ins where either you watch the car hops, read the menu on the board, or, if you have to face the other cars, at least feel you can look because of the windshield.

The coffee waitress came by his table to ask if he wanted a refill before she realized he hadn't gotten his dinner yet. He said, No, he was a tea-drinker, and she asked did that mean he didn't want coffee. He said, Yes, and while she poured him coffee he looked at her face with startled eyes I remembered. I half smiled at him, because of the waitress, but also because he couldn't know how close to remembering him I got when seeing eyes that went with a place.

Suddenly he called out, the sound of his voice startling me. I had watched his mouth begin to move before the words sifted through. "Where's your Bible?"

"Oh," came my voice, from the distance of that place. I rubbed my neck, trying to erase the creeping redness. I looked back up and raised my head higher than necessary. "I did that already. And ha! I see you didn't kill yourself either."

He smiled, more relaxed than me, I thought. "No, I'm selling spinners now."

"What are spinners?" I asked, sorry to have been drawn in by interest, but the mind has its own life and goes right on.

"Ah!" He jumped up and reached across the table to the bench opposite him and brought to the table top a large briefcase. He snapped the hinges and began pulling out a long rope, metallic, of red and silver which made a wind sound as it dropped to the floor.

"That," he said, "is a spinner. You string them up at used car lots and when the manager turns on the lights at night, they shine. Makes people notice. Wind, rain, sleet, heat of day, chill of night, nothing destroys them and they keep on shining. Makes people notice. They buy more cars that way." He drew the red and silver spinner into his hands and stuffed it back into the briefcase.

The waitress brought my plate first, and I resented the fact that his was on the same large tray. "Yours was chopped sirloin and crispy onion rings, right?" I wanted to ask her if she believed the crispy onion rings, but I caught myself. I have tried to stop doing things like that. It didn't get me anywhere. She asked him if his was chopped sirloin and crispy onion rings too, and he winked at me.

When she left, I held my fork in my hand, poised over the plate, and said, "Leave me alone, please."

He leaned over his plate, moving forward so that over the partition all I saw was his face too big, and whispered, "All you had to do that day was come in, just come in, and it would have been over. Kid." He raised his hands above the level of the booth and mimicked my hands clutched around the Bible, then slowly, in slow motion with grace, let his fingers move out and apart. His eyes followed the imaginary descent of the book to the floor. "Too bad," he said. "In fact, that's precisely why I didn't do it. I sat down on the sofa and said to myself, 'When the suicide squad sends out someone like *you* to save *me*, I got a mission in life.'"

I pushed back my plate, releasing the fork last, letting it twirl apart from the plate in the gravy of the sirloin. He was busy stirring another packet of sugar into the tea the waitress had silently eased onto his table. The ice cubes must have melted because I don't remember the clink. I would have heard it. I watched him until he sipped the tea.

"Spinners!" I said. I stood, pushing the cigarette pack into my pocket. My legs were bent at the knees because I hadn't moved away from the booth. "Listen," I said, "did it ever occur to you, just once, whether or not, whether. . . ." I stepped out into the aisle between the booths and tables-for-four. He didn't look surprised to see me moving toward him.

"What?" he asked.

My sandals felt tight, and I leaned over to loosen the buckles. He must have been watching me. "Christ," I said. "Never mind. Listen." I put my pointing finger on his table. "Listen, will you give me one of those spinners?" I reached into my pocket and brought out some change. "I'll pay you." I showed him the money and threw on the floor the silver paper torn from the cigarette package. The lady at the table next to the booth looked at me. I can always feel it when someone looks at me because I can feel my back get warm. I used to turn around when I felt my back get warm, but that way I found I never got to see the face, only the head ducking down, so now I wait and turn a little later. It's funny how their eyes stay the same, as if I had seen them immediately after. I forgot to look at this one, but I know anyway what she looked like.

The man watched the silver paper fly to the linoleum. "It's a demonstration model," he said. "If I let you have it, I'd have to tell my boss what happened. We only get one demonstration model a month. The rest we have to order."

"Aren't you going to ask why I want it?"

I could have asked that question in my mind except for the way words don't obey and come out too fast. I can remember how my mind asked that first and then knew it wasn't purposeful because it could see, the way I could see, that he wasn't going to ask exactly because he was interested. Maybe the mind likes a little order in spite of itself, or a justice of its own I don't understand.

I dropped the money back into my pocket and held it there with my left hand. "OK," I said, "it's really OK. And besides, I don't know about you. But I don't have to, you know. Today was a fluke. One rare thing. I won't see you again. Let it drop, I say."

I walked toward the register. I had to wait while the waitress came forward to tell the cashier what I had bought. "Wasn't the dinner to your liking?" she asked. They don't like strangers in the Melody; at least I know that now. Remember that, I said to myself. She wore a black, shiny apron, and her dress was dingy nylon-white. She was too thin and wasn't trying to please. If you work in a restaurant, I thought, food is what you stake it all on.

The register was in the center of the room, with booths lined on each wall and tables down the middle. I passed him as I left. He called out, ''The faces stay the same, honey. Only the names and occupations change.''

He didn't follow me home, which was probably just as well. I stopped first at the Hobby Shop for some hemp thread, orange-colored with silver threads running through. I wanted the spinner. I took the thread and put it in my pocket and drove home being glad he wasn't following. My neighbor snoops and wouldn't be able to imagine him being there.

When I first talked to her about writing him a letter, she thought it wouldn't work. One morning when I wanted to write a letter and couldn't think who to, I heard from the man on the radio. He called up on one of those interest shows which allows the listeners to discuss the topic of the day. The topic that day was suicide. He said he had been thinking about doing it. The ladies called after he talked, saying Pray and We love you, but I doubted it. Nobody sounded loving, and they talked about Christ, sounding mean.

My neighbor, when I told her, said, Who'd believe that, your letter, because it's easy to do. I don't know what she meant about easy to do. She has two prints of ballerina dancers on the longest wall in her dining room, and that seemed easy to do, or else very hard; I never figured. She moved the prints once and put them back a week later. I thought maybe she had washed the walls, but she said, No, she hated washing walls. But I didn't write him, because of what she said; she spoiled it. She said I didn't know what he looked like, and that I couldn't write him a personal letter if I couldn't know what he looked like. Things she says like that, in combination with the ballerina prints, is why I invite her over.

I knew what he looked like before she mentioned it. Five feet tall, skinny, thinning hair the way that's ugly, and nobody to find him sexy but himself and now it was hard to believe alone. One of the ladies who called to answer him said he should call the suicide squad at night if he thought about it, because the early morning hours were hardest since Christ had the hardest time then.

He must have called, because I called them and they said, Yes, I could go over if I first came down and took their training course. For a week. I asked them how they knew he wouldn't do it in a week, and they said the particular one didn't matter. I was in training for whoever called.

He called, one day at three forty-five in the afternoon, and when I got there, he didn't look like anything.

He kept the chain on the door, peeking through, and I saw him. When he closed the door to unchain it, I tried to peek through the spy hole, but the picture gets smaller on the wrong side of the door. He opened it, but I couldn't go in. He didn't argue, so I left. I told the Mission people about it, and they let me go, with the Bible for a memento.

He wouldn't like it here anyway. It bothers me, too, sometimes, with all the things around—scraps I collect. It gets too messy, and other times isn't messy enough. My neighbor doesn't mind any more, but the landlord asks me what if my husband comes back to that, what would he think, but I don't think he's coming back. I keep the windows open sometimes anyway, and with only the screen and no glass, he wouldn't mind too much. He knew I was trying to make something with the scraps. I pay the bills on time, so no one should worry.

I got some bottle caps last week and painted them with nail polish. They're the color of the hemp thread, almost. The biggest scrap is a piece of glass I had cut at the Pittsburg Plate Glass Company. I think I may try to glue the bottle caps onto the glass, or tie them to the thread, or maybe make a case for all the metal and mica bits I got on a visit to my sister's in Georgia and have the Glass Company bore holes in the glass for them to be tied through with the string.

I found an overcoat at Goodwill last week, and I may have to cut it up. On Fifth Street downtown, there's a man who wears a coat like that and pretends to shoplift. I've seen him three times. The man walks by with his long coat on, slowly and keeping his eyes straight ahead. Then his arm reaches out like a mechanical dummy and grabs a pair of socks or hose the owner keeps outside in bins for the fast shopper. Then the owner runs out from his place in the store, letting his chair he keeps tilted against a counter bang down, while his knees knock away the card table he does his calculations on. He runs out yelling, and the man in the overcoat moves his mechanical hand again and puts the socks or hose back and walks on. I followed him one time, but I noticed my shoulders got stiff and it was hard to follow as slowly as he walked.

That has happened when I have to ride the Fifth Street bus. On the same street there's a sign in pink fluorescent which says, FUNERALS BY LOWE and I always answer GLASS BY STEUBEN. But that isn't why, especially, I had the glass cut. Once, when my family—mother, sisters, me—was traveling around trying to find a living space, the trailer we carried came off the hitch. It was in the middle of Georgia. The sun was in the middle of the sky, and it happened right after we went over a railroad spar. Since the trailer was made of wood and cost twenty-five dollars second-hand, it split apart. We stopped the car and my mother said, My God, we could have been killed, and cried.

She didn't move the car, but no one was coming in another car. The only ones coming were black men who had been sitting on reunion camp chairs leaning against the side of a feed store. They walked close to the car and Mother said, Raise the window, quick! But they didn't look at us. They walked around the trailer saying, Lordy look a yonder, because the gold harp my mother had bought at an auction was shining in the sun and the Blue Willow china she had inherited crunched under their Navy surplus boots. The books had broken from their cases and there was no breeze to move the pages. It was hot. We watched them through the glass and no one opened a window to get help. When they finished looking, they opened the books that weren't thrown open and fingered the pages. One of the boys touched the harp, and we could hear it through the glass. Inside, we cried and watched until they came to our car and watched us. My mother told me one time that she and I were almost killed in a train when a passer-by at the station threw a rock against the train window where we were sitting and broke glass on us. I wasn't born yet, only a bulge in her stomach, and yet I remember the glass.

We must have been looking at the rock-thrower before he threw it. I would never go into one of those elevators on the outside of buildings made of glass so you can see your rise and descent. Lights of cities are like flecks of mica in a river, but you can't sift your hands through them. The Indians sew bits of glass on their dresses for some reason I have read about in books, but I wonder if, first, before that reason, they didn't bathe naked in rivers flowing with sand and come out flecked with silver and gold. I have imagined being flecked with silver and gold, naked. That would make me smile.

I should have told the man in the Melody, If the faces *don't* change, the occupations will stay the same. As for mine, I'm making something, and when I get it made, I'll give it to someone I care about, for a present.

The Love Child

Normally it would be dark outside when the girl began to brush her hair. She would loosen the braids, count the strokes to a hundred, and wait. If the hair were clean enough and shone, the mother would lean forward from her chair where the girl sat before her on the floor, and run a hand across the crown of the girl's head. Then she would turn to smile at the father.

The hair color and texture were inherited from his side of the family. Since the girl's mother loved the father, the smile meant approval of at least that, the hair. But never their religion with involved spasms of the body, tongue-twisting, sweat, and exhaustion; nor the "accidental" shootings which were sometimes deadly to strangers at pool rooms and the side rooms of bars where men played poker on Saturday nights; nor any of the red milk glass they collected—"blood-red," the mother said, "Christ-blood-red"; nor any photographs, in any pose, the family together or apart, because, the mother said, when you died they took those pictures closer to the window-light than they had been before, and, looking, they made up lies about the face and the posture and the amount of sin in the bowels.

The mother did not talk this way to the father. With him she became stubborn—the mouth made an "o" and the tongue could be seen flicking up, and the word "no" would come out like no other word. And that was why the father loved the mother; with her he might die clean—clean the way china is clean, and glassware from Italy, and sterling silver, and the insides of Packard cars.

But now the mother had gone down the road with the woven pocketbook he had brought her from a trip near Mexico. The pocketbook had been stuffed with crackers, three pairs of hose, two of nylon see-through panties, and a diploma from a woman's college which required its girls to wear navy blue and to play at least one musical instrument. She had been gone long enough for the crackers to have been eaten, long enough for the girl to have sewn nineteen pieces of different-colored material into a shape almost square.

It was the girl's idea that if she made a quilt for her mother, her mother would come back, and, more than that, she would return on the day the quilt was finished. The girl sewed during all the daylight hours, and the day before, she had gone into the kitchen of the Barnard sisters on the adjoining property and had stolen a candle. In the sisters' oven had been three biscuits and a slab of cornbread. While looking in at the bread, the girl remembered what she had read about the religious act of fasting. The act meant the body was an instrument of power if it looked a certain way and if others could see it would look worse unless that thing you wanted changed was changed. She had shut the oven door and had begun a fast, and although she had been hungry for days, her hunger was suffusive now.

It would have been normal, too, for the girl to think very little. Instead, she would run in the woods alone, and pretend stories from books, and jump over rails which she built from fallen limbs, and sing loudly.

Now she had thoughts. They came slowly, and they came in sentences that seemed to belong to a person who was stupid. Inside the house, she felt as if she knew exactly what she were doing with each minute, but a sense of other time was lost.

Lately, too, she had begun to make up love songs, trying to imitate a record she had heard before the radio went bad. Slurring her words as she thought Kitty Kallen might, she imagined a man was in the control room adjusting the whispers up or down. In death, she thought, the eyes could talk, and so they put pennies on the eyes to keep the voice down with the body.

The house faced West, so the bedrooms darkened first, after the trees. At the time the woods darkened, the girl would come in and see the father sitting where she had left him, in the one arm chair of blue material, sitting near the picture window. At this hour he would appear aflame from the sun going down. The starched collar of his shirt would appear pink, and the ruby eyes of the tiny shakes which were on the cuff links would blaze orange. His navy suit would look purple, the color of dragonfly wings. And his eyes, changed from pale blue to brown, would appear enormous.

He had given up talking altogether. When she stepped past him it was like going past a painting. Yet she had been told by her mother that the purpose of stories was to keep alive what people wanted to forget, and that what seemed dead was actually in a waiting state, like, she said, a man who wanted to love a woman, or like a baby, in a womb with a face no one had seen, anxious to surprise. The man contained stories precisely because he explained nothing, and his face seemed new.

He looked out the picture window as she brushed and held the hair up in the sun until the strands were amber. As the sun moved across the room, she moved with it, near him by the eightieth stroke. It was August; the sun would move faster now.

"I'm hungry," she whined, and he turned to see her holding strands of hair in her mouth. When she had seen that he saw, she turned a somersault on the linoleum. "My stomach is *flat*," she said, pressing both hands on it. "When I roll, it's a plate, a tiny empty plate. It may break."

"You're too big to do that," he answered. "Go do something else."

The girl bit her lips; he was not only talking but looking. She held her bottom lip with her teeth until he turned away. "She may die, you know." She brushed and counted, "Eighty-one, eighty-two," and dropped the brush on the floor. "Robbers may come along, and since she hasn't any money— except she may get pennies for some Coke bottles if she thinks of it while she walks—they'll take her back to where they live in a cabin and make her cook for them. And they won't mind her eating too, *when* they're done, but they won't *get* done, so it won't be like here, where there's nothing. It will be like: there's a lot but no time to eat, so, so her own skin could fall in the pot, you know."

She waited.

The sun was past them, his eyes were blue again like satin-weight. At last she went to the bedroom and sewed by the leavings of light, and she tried to think.

The bedroom was the width of three twin beds, but since they needed only one for themselves and one for the girl, the man had suspended a rod above the space where the third might have gone, and on the rod he had hung his suits, with the mother's washdresses at one end, and the girl's Sunday dress at the other end, near the window, to keep it bleached white, and to keep the sun off his suits.

His suits were heavy, and when the mother had been home to make noise in the bedroom, the suits muffled the sounds. If the girl wanted to hear more, she lifted the arms of the suits, and gathered them in her hands, and held on to them.

The beds were handmade, by the father. He liked what he owned to be either good or handmade. He had built each bed of six oak planks, two solid planks for the sides and four cut into narrow strips to go on top to hold the mattress. The beds were heavy, silent, and, underneath, dark.

On this night he talked, she took her scraps, her candle, and herself, and put them all in the corner, where the bed met the wall. After wrapping the bottom of the candle in a scrap of cloth, she put the candle between the big and second toe of one foot. While sewing, she tried to let only her fingers move. When she finished sewing the twentieth piece on the quilt, she scraped the wax from the material. Peeling off the wax made her think of sealing wax she had seen in stationery stores one summer they had visited stores. Finally, this wax made her think of the letters which were in boxes underneath the mother's and the father's bed. With what was left of the candle, she looked beneath the bed. The mother had shoved the boxes near the head of the bed, very far back, so the girl blew out the candle and crawled.

It was smelly; dust covered the floor, but the boxes were clean inside plastic bags. The girl opened the bags, then the shoe boxes emptied of his shoes. She imagined the colors of the ribbons: soft-yellow, blue, satin-brown, and pink. She tilted a box close to her nose, breathing in the mixture of perfumes. Then, although she didn't want to, she fell asleep.

In a dream, he and she were in her grandfather's house where the sunlight made everything of wood appear soft. She went from room to room with her hands out, as if the autumn colors and smells were like wheat to be scooped up. When she was in the smallest room, off the kitchen porch, she saw a man in a cape heading around the back of the house to the front. She began tightening the locks on all the windows and closing those open, running and calling to the father, "I'm closing them, but he's coming around *there!*" She didn't see the father; rather, he felt present, until she came to the last small room. There, inside the room, in the only dark corner, the man sat with his knees pulled toward his chest.

His body appeared small. She sat beside him as if he were her size. Her shoulders touched the cape, and beneath the cape, she felt the bones move. His eyes were dark, and in the half-light, they appeared sad to the girl. She reached out to touch his arm which he held next to his stomach, between his chest and the legs pulled close. When she touched the arm, it seemed that hours had passed, and when he spoke, it was as if she knew his voice. "Love," he said, turning to pull out his arm, "you have made me love," and he held up his palm to show her the hole and the blood.

In the morning, she woke with the dream still present, and in her confusion, she reached out to wipe the hand. Instead, she touched the boxes, and pulled two toward her chest. She inched out, trying to be soundless. She saw as she passed him that he was awake, in the same position in which she had left him. A thought, that she ought to wave, came to her; instead, she let the door slam while she ran to the Packard.

The Packard was sitting on concrete blocks because the tires were still good, and he had visions one day of their having gas with which to run the car again. He had talked at the beginning of summer of taking them to a museum; often then he went out to check the tires, to dust the hood and its silver eagle.

The girl balanced herself on one block and leaned forward to open the back door. Then she jumped down and threw the boxes up on the grey wool-covered seat. The heat from inside the car hit her face, and she climbed in to it and the boxes, locking all the doors and tightening the windows. She read until afternoon.

The lady she liked best was named Nina. Three years before, Nina had written to the father every day for two weeks. Nina did not sprinkle her letters with perfume, nor enclose a photograph, nor ask him for one, nor invite him to her house. In the fourteen letters, she wrote the same thing, in many different ways: "I do not normally write letters to strangers. In fact, I rarely listen to the radio. I had not expected to find myself in this beggar's position as a woman. I say 'beggar's' not because I want anything which I can define. I ask only that you allow me to write to you without your thinking of me as desperate. Perhaps it will help my cause if I tell you that, after listening to you for many weeks, I do not believe you like reading Elizabeth Barrett Browning poetry to the strains of 'Ebb Tide' in the background. I suspect you despise the style of the Melachrino Strings. In fact, I think all that you like about your program is that you do it well, what you do. I suspect you can be cruel. Nina."

He had moved, and she missed his voice. Or he had moved and she continued to write without his voice. Or he sometimes went where she was, or something had happened to her, or to him. Any of this was possible, she thought.

It was possible, too, that he would come to the car. Now it seemed to the girl that she had waited for him the whole day, to appear at one window or another, to look in, and with the car on blocks, his head would come just to the windows, and he might have to jump up to see her lying on the seat.

The sun began to light the picture window. It began to glow red—she thought of how paper beneath a prism's light burned. But the house did not burn, he did not come out, it got cold in the car. She let loose her hair. Holding it around her shoulders, she half-slept, to make more waiting easier.

Later, in a state of dreaminess, she went inside the house, when the moon was up, the crickets asleep in a quiet they had let happen. The screen door scraped on the stone steps, and he turned to look at her. She walked past him, to the bedroom door. He watched, and when she looked quickly at him to make certain he was watching still, she smoothed down her dress. She understood now that the lack of food had made her smaller; the dress moved under her fingers.

"I feel like Nina," she said.

When she turned and threw herself on the bed and covered herself with the sheet, she heard him get up. He came to the bed, he reached down, and shook her shoulders, but she wouldn't move. They were like that in the room for what seemed to the girl to be a long time. When he turned away, she heard him opening the cabinet doors in the kitchen, and she listened until she was too tired to listen.

It was very dark inside the room when she heard him call her name twice, then the name "Nina." She turned to see his shape in the doorway, his gun in one hand, a back pack in the other. She got up slowly, and when she was even with him at the doorway, she saw from the living room light that he had washed his face, straightened his tie, and put on his hunting boots of soft red leather. "Hey," he said, "we're going to hunt us a rabbit and eat. I promise."

She found her shoes and a sweater and followed him out the front, to the side, past the car, and into the woods. He carried a lantern, and she followed, not the light but the shape of his head above the pack on his back. Nothing seemed to move but their feet. No rabbit would come out for this.

She followed him to a clearing where she had beaten a path once while trying to jump over the rails she had made. In the softest grass, he pushed on her shoulders until she sat. She watched how he built the fire carefully, first digging a hole in the earth for safety. When the clearing seemed bright with fire, he went into the trees. She watched the fire and listened for the one shot.

Before that shot, the woods were more still than she remembered they could be, as if the breath of every animal held. Then the shot, the sound of his feet going away, and returning. He came to the clearing with the rabbit limp in his hands, bloodless.

He cooked in a pot he had brought, and he spread a cloth in front of her, and on the cloth he put two china plates, and beside the plates their silver initialed with his letters. He shined two silver goblets on the tail of his shirt, and poured into each the wine they had made when there was sugar in the house.

Often he turned from the cooking meat to smile at her. He spread the empty knapsack on the ground before he sat to carve the rabbit with their carving knife. Handing her the plate, he said, "Eat, eat."

At first when she picked up the fork, it was as if she had forgotten how. She said, "*She* won't be eating."

"Women always eat, *always*. Don't you know that by now? They find a way to eat."

When she began to eat, it was as if she might never stop. She ate what he had put on her plate, letting the juice drip down on her dress, and some blood because he had cooked it too fast, and then she reached to take meat from his plate. He laughed, and leaned over to put a hand on her head. He rubbed her hair, saying, "Lady, you lady."

Then, suddenly, she stood and began to vomit, near her plate and almost splashing him. But he jumped when it seemed she might fall. He came to her and held her, with one hand on her stomach pressing down, until she was empty again. He lifted her and laid her near the fire, and took off his jacket and spread it around her, tucking it in, smoothing down her dress, her hair.

She dozed while he carried her, going slowly so that she felt a rocking against her ribs, the coldness of his shirt, the wool of his jacket across her back, nothing between him and her but the shirt, its buttons rubbing on her dress as he walked. She thought she could not waken all the way again.

When he put her on the bed, she imagined herself talking to him. She kept her eyes closed, but moving her face upward so that she might talk if she decided. When her head was turned, he began stroking her face, the eyebrows, the line of her nose, her ears. It was almost the way her mother stroked, but the girl noticed she was becoming more awake behind her eyes, as if she *were* looking at him, while her arms and legs seemed to sleep separately, sinking deeper into the mattress, apart and adrift.

He pulled the sheet from these arms and legs, and he found the stomach between, and began feeling the bones, the space between the bones, the ribs, the neck, a humming coming from his chest while he rubbed, the humming going out when he touched the flatness of her chest, and found the nipples without fat.

Later, without knowing why, she sat up and rocked his head in her lap. When it began to brighten above her head, he went out, and before she slept, she heard him slide into his chair, and soon after, his snoring.

Finally, the mother was walking down the road. The girl heard a car door slam, the engine start up again, the flats of her shoes on the gravel, with silence where the red dust was. The mother began calling; she called five times, then the girl heard her running, and at the porch, the sound of bags dropping. The mother threw open the screen and looked.

They were like this: the father in the chair, looking out the window almost as he had been when the mother took off walking. The girl was sitting near the chair but to the left, with her back against the wall so the only thing visible of the father from where the girl sat was his head showing above the blue of the chair. The girl was looking at his head, and only on either side of his head at the sky outside.

The mother's face appeared large, her nose sniffing. She looked at them, from one to the other, again and again. The girl saw her mother shake, and then it must have been that the mother caught hold of that motion on purpose. She shook herself again, her whole head, then she turned and stepped out again. The girl heard the mother walk off, then the sound of her steps, returning.

"I'm home!" she called. "And look what I got!"

And the mother came bursting into the room. She went to the girl and opened the bag and showed her: bacon, cheese, bread, lettuce, tomatoes, butter, canned meat, coffee, and two packages of Kool-Aid. "And more in the other bag!" she said. "Now help me in the kitchen and we'll cook up a feast."

She pulled the father's arm until he sat down beside the girl, across from the mother. "We'll skip the blessing this time," she said, "so dig in." She passed them food, again and again, while she talked very fast of the relatives of hers she had seen, and the job she might have, and how it was to go to the curb market. She made the girl eat until the girl's face began to move in a way the mother was accustomed to. "Ha!" she said, reaching across to poke the girl's stomach. "We'll get you fat again, and roses in those cheeks," and she tickled the girl's ribs until the girl laughed. After they had cleared the table, the mother noticed the piece of quilting which the girl had spread on the table. The mother touched it and said, "Pretty. We like things pretty, don't we?"

Now the mother grew silent. After the dinner, she never talked of having been gone. She never asked how they had been. The father asked for salt at meals, and if there was no bread on the table, he pushed back his chair loudly and said, "Shit-Christ, can't you remember the bread to *push* with?"

And they couldn't get the father to move, to help carry the furniture to the U-Haul she rented. So they carried it themselves, only the mother didn't ask for the chair, even though she could have carried it alone.

When they pulled out, the mother stopped the truck on the road by the metal mailbox, to leave a note for the carrier. Together they turned to look at the house, so the way they remembered him best was encased and waiting, and with a face which would surprise.

The Virgin

Roselle, the music teacher, was one of those rare women about whom nothing bad was said.

When her mother died, Roselle wasn't tired from all the nursing, nor bitter. This only relation deserved, if anyone, death—pain having been the usher.

Roselle had a print shop make up for her a hundred little cards, like calling cards, on which the words "PIANO LESSONS: REPUTABLE" had been centered in Roman Bold, above her name in Florence script.

She had something of a name—more a legacy from her mother's concert career than of her own making, although in her late twenties, Roselle had been appreciated at the Baldwin in such places as Denver and Tanglewood. Most of the parents who called for their children's sake didn't, however, know the tradition to which she belonged. They wanted "a few lessons to off-set the effects of T.V." or, as one woman put it, "By God, just to get her out of the house on Saturday, if you know what I mean." Which Roselle didn't. "And why shouldn't I?" the mother asked. "*How much?*"

The children loved Roselle, or, as Roselle knew, they loved Beethoven and Bach and Chopin (never Rachmaninoff). In her living room, with her pupils, Roselle became expansive. She rubbed her children's hair and clipped their nails and moaned dramatically, "Oh Lubchkin, Beethoven would die if he heard that!"

The children would say, "He's dead. *We* know that."

Then Roselle would sit up very straight, wash the smile off her face with an open palm, and, giving a loud stage sigh, say, "Ah, but you see, that is the thing: musicians like him, they die but they keep *listening*. And when it's awful, it's like a fingernail scraped down your spine. Poor man."

And, especially, they loved "The Moonlight Sonata." Its simplicity like, she told them, a curtsy before The Queen, which tells, without revealing just why, what province of grace you came from and how far you might go.

At recital time, Roselle had printed up on cream-colored paper "Beethoven: Opus 27, No. 2," with the names of her dozen best students alphabetically arranged down the right, inside page. Once a year, with Roselle sitting among them, the parents listened to twelve renderings of the Adagio Sostenuto, and had not each pupil convinced his parents that this recital was the most important thing in their little worlds, the parents might have found the recital peculiar.

As it was, the parents sat composed on the rented folding chairs surrounding the grand piano and, having been arrested by seeming repetition, gave themselves over to it. They discovered a brilliance, or two.

"How much?"

Roselle got for herself what was possible to get, and who could say, exactly, that he was For or Against. Like being confronted with the Latin language, or death at its awesome moment. If she were water, one might on a Saturday afternoon test: viscosity.

But Roselle is a woman, age 39.

When someone asks Roselle her age, at insurance companies and doctors' offices, she says, "Thirty-nine" with a slight question in her voice, as if to ask, Does this mean something I don't know about? Discount death: her mother had loved her, as simply as that, and her father, who no doubt loved her as well, had died when Roselle was three. So Roselle's raised voice was innocent. These men or women who took down her statistics would be ashamed to look up then, as if one glance might loosen her, like a sawed limb ready to fall one way or another.

Her apartment is all her own: no one throws her out because no one gathers her in. The rooms are big, with polished floors and flowers on the sills and bright red rugs. The only complaint to make is, not that it is far from where she and her mother lived the early part of their lives together; rather, in the summer, with the windows open, the ambulances, whining their ways through the street, can interfere with the metronome's ticking: *him & her, him & her.*

Roselle's mother *breathed* in that hospital, her lungs attached to a machine, the machine, not she, going in and out, in and out, a passion of unlike bodies which couldn't last, though to have it was why Roselle had brought her mother to this town. And the piano, the sheet music, the good clothes.

And now Roselle herself is ill.

Once, on her way to a music store (walking because she has no car and doesn't buy one since she cannot imagine herself learning how to drive), Roselle walked inside a convalescent hospital. A clean building inside which nothing fast was happening. On the first floor, where the paper work was done, no one stopped her, to ask if she were lost. She didn't look lost, carried along on impulse—another set of impeccable hands. (Outside and rounding the corner which holds the hospital, it is a sense of her future which makes her feet fly, her body push against the movable walls of leaves falling, as if by going into their motion, she is straining herself cleaner and cleaner.)

She went up and down the corridors, hands still in her red coat pockets, the paisley scarf still knotted at her neck. At the end of a long hall, someone came out of an office—an associate of someone inside, since he nodded and said, "At lunch, then." She was curious: for what man would another man close the door so softly? Roselle leaned herself against the cool metal wall opposite this door and waited, to see this man. And, when no one came to see him on business in the time that she had, Roselle herself knocked, twice, very quietly.

And when he called, "Come in," Roselle, in a languid motion unlike herself, stretched one leg and gave the door a push. He was eating cake, a dark, chocolate cake, with nuts laced through and scattered, browned, on the top.

He should have said something; it was his mistake. People in offices live in a certain order: it is up to them to speak when someone like Roselle looks in with no nameable business. But he didn't, not even in the longest minute that constituted their looking, mutual and of similar disorder.

If she, later, justified herself, it was to say, The cake: someone makes him that kind of cake. So, beforehand, I knew how it would be.

Roselle was 34 then.

He let her come back; that is, she came back, each time on her way to sort through the new music at the store where she traded, and on impulse, until, not knowing what else to do with her, he touched her. Beginning with the ears. The kind of man who can have his associates know they knock before entering, so there is no point in locking the door, cake or no cake.

Is this love?

Austere, Roselle, later, flips through the sheet music and amazes herself with how little shows, or the man who sells her music every week would turn, suddenly, when she isn't paying attention, and look at her, newly.

"Do you think he sees you on me?" she asks this man who touches her.

"I'm quite sure he does," he answers, laughing. "I show."

And yet: he only rearranged her clothes, and his own pin stripes, even on the sixth or eighth visit when, seemingly, for Roselle, there should come a time when she does not gauge herself by the man in the music store, but takes herself home, for a bath.

In the hospital, they bathed her mother daily, with green sponges, and, toward the end, three times daily, a lorgnette for watching death come.

He smoothed her dress—her lover did—and his own embroidered shirt down around his waist, tight, over which the vest lay—to Roselle he was a beautiful man—and sat her opposite him, across the wide desk, her head, from where she sank in the leather chair, a bouy.

"Roselle," he said, "I'm a rich man, pretty rich, which I tell you so you'll understand what I say next. That is," he said, "I am about to tell you a fact, unrelated to the above, namely, honey, I can't afford you. That's it," he said.

Cloven.

In her sunny rooms, Roselle wrapped herself with her own arms and mended herself with her own arms and asked herself: given music, what did I do wrong?

Seeing her for the first time, the father of her best pupil thought, "At the minimum, it would take, say, walking right up and surprising her—one hand on each breast, with no introduction," his own surmise a breach. Once, when Roselle took his little girl to hear Lorin Hollander play at the music hall, he gave Roselle a ride to the bus stop. Watching her walk away from his car, he got out to call, "I'd better drive you home. Something might happen." And, maybe, she missed death by seconds.

How much?

And, on this particular morning, Roselle, who gauged herself by her fingers, beginning at the temple and down the cheeks and to her neck where the pulse was, saw, at her collar bone, a knot, plum-size, *it* pulsing, quarter-time like a drum.

At the hospital, they asked Roselle: Think back—it's very important. Do you remember ever seeing something like a sack of skin hanging down on one of your relatives' necks? A woman? A cousin, an aunt, your grandmother. . . .

"What *is* it?"

"Think," they said.

"Once," Roselle said, "I think I was three—it was with my father—we went to see my grandmother. I'd never been there before. Her room was blue, a bright royal blue. My father came in behind me; he had some cloth in his hands, cloth that same color. Grandmother was in her bed by the window. I remember she hugged me, then she looked back out the window. And my father took the material over to a chair and held it up to the chair, measuring. My grandmother turned from the window—I didn't know her well—and she said something to me. I saw some things on her tongue. So I walked over to her. They were bubbles, four of them, and they moved when she talked, as if they were filled with milk, and, from the milk, the color of the room was on the bubbles." Roselle asked them, "Is that what you mean? I mean, that shade of blue. . . . I haven't seen that color of blue since then."

The doctors patted Roselle's hand; they said, "No." And, "Never mind. We'll do some tests."

No one could call her music students but herself, so, in the hall, she called them. A nurse gave her a key—for her clothes—"even the rings"—and a gown to put on before going beneath the machine, which was to count a body-substance and tell them what they needed to know about her relations she couldn't remember. "Do I have to be cleaned beforehand?" she asked.

The machine told them nothing, as machines in hospitals often do, as with her mother, when the air pump quit before her mother quit, and her mother turned black, as if in rage. They said it would have happened, one time or another, and they closed her eyes to erase the rage.

For Roselle, they flew a specialist in, who felt and said to the men around her on the consultation table, "What do you need, a map? It's a fist. So cut it out." They took out of her the food they had let her put in herself that morning and they gave her a shot and, inside the circle of lights, they cut loose the fist and sewed her up.

A thin, thin scar. Roselle's doctor said, "I'm proud of it. You're as pretty as ever." He looked at her. "You do know you're pretty, don't you?" Am I, Roselle asked. Really?

For her rest and to clean and to supervise the students who would come to practice while she corrected them from her bed, Roselle called the convalescent hospital, for nurse's aides. They sent her by bus a pair of cousins—squat, efficient women with white uniforms whose bodice-tucks looked sharp enough to clean fingernails on. They talked over her bed and around her bed and back and forth from the windows they dusted.

They gave the children candy, Roselle calling them in, saying, "Candy!

You can't concentrate with candy! Do it again, sticky-fingers," and she received the candy into her palm covered with a layer of Kleenex.

The cousins said, "Raymond got laid off last week."

"Is that so?"

"That's the second time this month."

"Well . . . ."

Yet, it was clean—a pastiche of sunlight around her, music, clean sheets. The cousins were old women unaccustomed to her. They lifted the busts and they asked, "Who's he?" and they fed her soup as if she were china. Yet it was clean. "You're doing fine!" the cousins said, as if she were other-than-them, a doily freshly starched and laid on a chair arm.

"Play fortissimo," Roselle shouted into the living room. But the cousins who nursed her didn't get a hint. They discovered Roselle's two nightgowns, full of tiny holes, lace-bare, ragged at the necks, without color.

"Look," they said, pointing above her, one on either side.

"You wouldn't believe it," they said.

"No," they said, "who would have thought?"

Roselle covered herself, remembering, "I gave my good ones to my mother, for when she was ill." Remembering: "No, those were hers." Laughing, "Well, I *am* a mess, aren't I?"

They nodded, one on each side, hands clasped, agreeing. "So get yourself some new ones. One of us will go buy them. Some with lace, some flowers, a rose-bud at the neck."

Roselle kissed the last music student goodbye, waving with a peppermint-flecked Kleenex. The cousins cleaned up after the children while Roselle dozed, her curtains parted, sunlight at the ledge.

Waking to one of the cousins coming in on crepe soles, on her way to the kitchen, Roselle said, "I remember seeing a film in French once, a peasant film. The girls wore the whitest gowns. Hand-made. Thick material, the narrowest tucks. Soft—the camera light looked blue, it was such soft material. I'd like some like that."

"Like that?" the cousin said.

"Old-fashioned?" the other said, coming in.

"Like Oscar and Paul make," the other answered. "In Michigan," she explained to Roselle. "On the island."

"We could order you some," they told her.

So Roselle let them hold her up and measure her height and the width across her shoulders, and the neck-size, higher than the scar, plus room for lace. "Hand-made?" Roselle asked.

"Oh yes," they said. "And on the island, nothing but horses and people. Snow. Oh: hand-made."

As if they had worn her out, Roselle sent the cousins away, having gotten the address of their cousins' little tailor shop on the island. She let the students come as usual. She stayed in bed, writing the note in which she ordered the gowns, adding the postscript that she would pick them up herself. And writing the notes to each student, telling him how long she would be gone—only two weeks—and what pieces to have ready to play when she returned. It took a week, for the notes and, presumbably, for their sewing.

She called the hospital, and the cousins returned, even though she had asked for either one, to help her to the station and onto the seat, her bags within easy reach. They kissed her, one on each cheek. "Thank you!" Roselle called, and they waved to her through the train window—two persevering women with still-dark hair, rosied cheeks.

It would not be long—seven hours, no change, a reservation made by phone for a room after the trip, the short carriage trip, the side-trip to the tailors' shop for the gowns, then sleep.

In Lansing, it begins to snow. She sleeps.

The porter helps her to the cab and the cabbie helps her to the ferry, and on the island, the ferry man helps her to the carriage, and the carriage man takes her to the shop, although, he warns her, it is after six o'clock and they will be gone—the Niebor Brothers, cousins, really, he tells her, "craftsmen like we all are," he says. "Even me," he tells Roselle, smiling back to her.

The shop lights are on, and Roselle takes herself down, telling her carriageman to wait. The lights are kerosene and flicker in the wind of the door opening. Roselle goes slowly and finds them in the back.

"It's you," these similar cousins say. "We waited. You're late, you know."

Roselle is flustered, like a spring leaf. "I know. I'm sorry," she says. "It snowed and I expect that is what slowed us down."

"Snow?" one says to the other.

"No," he answers, "not here. Snow never slows us down here, does it?"

Roselle laughs. "No, I expect not. But have you got my gowns ready? I didn't bring any others. Your cousins laughed at me, seeing what I had, so I thought before I went on . . . ."

"Ready?" they ask each other. "Certainly," and the shortest one gives Roselle her package wrapped in brown paper.

"Do you mind if I open it here," she says, "to see . . . ."

"Us?" they ask. "Not us."

Roselle feels the softness of the material—just as in the film—and smiles while she pulls the whole, long gowns out, their tiny hand-sewn tucks catching in the paper, then sliding out. The tiny buttonholes, the hand-made lace at the neck.

"Oh! Beautiful! I love them both," she cries, and holds them up to her and twirls in front of the cousins, her hand at her neck, holding them up.

They smile.

"Flowers?" Roselle asks. "Do I see flowers? You embroidered flowers—all over? Oh! I love them. All over?!" And she turns the gowns around to see yards of flowers. "Mine?" she asks them. "You shouldn't have," she says. "It must have taken all your time—they're so tiny and delicate and . . . ."

The carriage driver comes to the door. He asks, "Miss? You'll be coming soon?"

"Oh yes," she answers. "And look! Flowers." She holds up the gowns for him to see. "I feel well already. I'll be right there."

Roselle folds her gowns and lays them on the wrapping paper. "I thank you kindly," she says. "Was the check adequate?"

"Machine," one of the cousins says. "By machine."

"The flowers," the other cousin says. "He means only the flowers."

"You mean the flowers are not hand-made?" Roselle asks. "But *why?*"

"We decided ourselves. We decided by phone, talking. An adjustment we made on our own, with our cousins."

"What?" Roselle asks.

They laugh. "We decided." One taps a pencil on his teeth. "And why not? You didn't order flowers, so we had the right to decide how to decorate, right?" He taps his cousin's belly.

"Right!" they say, laughing, "right!" And they both laugh and tap their pencils on their teeth as Roselle runs to the carriage, her gowns coming loose and flapping around her arms.

But: she had paid $17.00 for each one. She didn't waste them. And they were heavy and warm, so, in her gowns, she wrapped her arms around herself, and slept.

At breakfast, in the hotel, some people noticed her, sitting alone.

By the supper meal, some had noticed her and had thought about her.

And, in a day or so, a few men, watching Roselle, her long clean fingers and the half-moons of her nails which shone on the slightly shaking cup—they decided of her: she, maybe, had been loved. But not well. No, not well.

And, watching her, they had images of walking up to her. A smile, her raised neck, the uncertain mouth.

Of how it might be to say hello and to offer to sit.
And, even, of, one night, taking her out.
And, even, of the eventual appraisal of love-making.
And, even, perhaps love.

Feet

During the months of the Korean War, Louise, a mother of 39, and Josie, her eleven-year old daughter, lived in Pelzer, South Carolina. Across from the railroad tracks, mill children waited on their porches at dusk for their parents to come home. Lined up, their heads made steps. Until the mill closed long after the war was over, this scene was recurring. Nothing appeared to change, but because the two service station owners built almost identical asbestos-siding homes during that time, Louise and Josie would come to think the pale shades of green and pink belonged to war-time.

The mother and the child did not keep track of the number of men the newspaper reported were falling in the war. There was no way to tell how many of those who had wanted to die had died, or how many of those who had not wanted to die had died, or how many who had shot off their own toes in their back yards with shotguns were sick to death of not wanting to die.

Still, there was consolation in the field of daisies across from the house. Years later, when Louise and Josie would happen to go as tourists to the cemetery in Arlington, Virginia, they would feel betrayed by white crosses looking so much like a field of daisies.

But now, the mother, who slept on a day bed in the living room, woke each morning to spend five minutes looking out the window to the field where the slightest wind moved a thousand heads. And Josie, from her window, was looking too—the single eyes of yellow, blinking. In winter, they were apparitions, in memory, all white.

Where was the father, the husband?
He was dead.

In the space Louise's husband once occupied were piles of ladies' magazines, of underwear, boxes, and an empty space on the day bed where the second pillow used to be. The odor of woman was like a third person. They knew he would hate the house arrested in this mess, and their knowledge of his hatred was another odor.

Often over meals Louise said to Josie of their cousin four times removed, "If Harry gets back without getting himself blown to smithereens, we'll clean this place up and throw him a wham-bam party, whatcha say?"

Josie nodded. And Harry did get home much later and they did clean up and throw him a party, but he had lost too much sense to notice and sat in an armchair, waving.

Saturdays, to make time meet, Louise gave violin lessons to a girl Louise said was hopeless. Louise made Josie take lessons with the girl. "You play decent," Louise told Josie. "Keep my interest up." Between Josie and the girl, they made Louise concentrate, all songs in three-quarter time.

Sundays they went to church and liked each other in the pews better than they liked each other in the house because in church they sang, one soprano, one alto, and there was no question who would sing which part since nature had sealed in each a particular range. Afterwards they ate chicken, and it was fortunate that Louise liked the breast and Josie liked the inner part of the wing.

On Sundays, too, Charlie, Harry's father, came visiting, even though he did not present himself but parked his car below the rise in the road or behind the cluster of trees, and when he could hear Louise and Josie cooking in the kitchen or pulling the shades for their naps, he wrote messages in the dirt of their drive with a stick. One Sunday he would write: I WAS HERE. The next he would follow with WHERE WERE YOU? Or, he would ask, DON'T YOU LADIES EVER STAY HOME? And follow that with GOD IS LOVE.

Josie waited to see HARRY DIED, even though Charlie was a dairy farmer and would never think to write a message like that.

Other days of the week, Louise taught music in the Anderson County Public Schools, schools clustered on the map in the kitchen like shoes under a bed. When Louise first began to teach, she got lost on the country roads and came home crying, her autoharp vibrating on the kitchen table where she dropped it. Now she knew where to go. Every child in the county could play a song on the autoharp. They sang along, "Whispering hope, o how welcome thy voice," and when they had the whole song straight, Louise set the autoharp down on the table so gently not a string moved, and said she was bored to tears.

Would he ever come back?
No.

Louise grew a layer of fat almost translucent as a batiste baptismal dress on a girl who has waited too long to be saved—under the minister's hands and under the minister's robe: water, a prophecy: the body is so tender it falls in time from the bone.

Josie refused to get saved. She took walks in the woods and practiced being a ballerina who does not need toe shoes.

Harry wrote almost everyone was dead. "P.S.," he added, "not me," and Charlie drove all the way up their drive to say "Thank God" in Louise's hearing range. Charlie learned, in time, to celebrate by playing checkers in the silence Harry afterwards required, and went ahead and invested in automatic milking machines, contributing to the post-war boom.

Louise rented. While her husband would not come back, there was in life always the outside chance. Women who bought their own homes did not understand men. Relatives at the Easter reunion said she would be a renter all her life and they said she would have to stop pretending to be so young if Josie was going to look like that: legs toned and eyes toned down.

Because it was a custom, Louise and Josie took to the reunion a cake they had baked for the oldest living relation, who said she would *not* die, yellow cake crumbs sticking to her lips like pollen, her insides, they said, absolutely in shreds.

"Who does she think she *is?*" Louise asked, and they forgave her because of him.

When he was alive, what did he do?
A little of this and that; in bed, the other.

It was what he had been best at that had left Louise house-poor. This one sat at the front of a field. Far back were the railroad tracks, trains keeping so closely to a schedule Louise felt it as an affront. *He* had taught her to be ready at any time, and then, in those days, if two small boys had put their ears to her chest, between the breasts on the flat bone, they would have heard a humming; they would have jumped back as if they might get run over. Now two boys who were almost men came over on Saturdays to cut the grass, and they wouldn't have thought, looking at her, of whistling. No one knew that flat bone had once almost split like a tie.

And then, at the height of summer, when Louise's teeth itched, the landlord showed up. It was his house, his door and windows and clustered trees. And, in a way, it was his music trying to float from the house and not making it all because Louise, in a fit, had said Josie and the girl would, if it killed *her*, learn to play Mendelssohn's Violin Concerto, and the girl's father, who waited in the car in the drive, sent in $2.50 instead of the usual three, not hearing in Louise's lessons the tremolo of hope.

New fat on Louise's upper arms quivered; she rubbed too much rosin on the bow and still, in the heat, it dried out. Josie got slapped on her bare legs so many times so softly that Louise's hand on her legs was a counter-rhythm.

Into all that, the landlord came, and he wasn't anything like the husband, the father.

Was he, in his day, what they call a 'natural'?
Louise had put the pillow at the foot of the bed and hooked her toes on the headboard. That helped.

The landlord knocked one Saturday during a music lesson. The external view would have made neighbors think of a Jehovah's Witness without a partner—the suit, the arranged hair, the valise.

Josie and the girl who did everything a second too late rested their violins on the metal music stand. They heard mumbling and their own white blouses rubbing on their shoulders, then Louise crying out, "You are kidding."

He wasn't. He walked past the space heater and through the space where french doors once hung and past Josie and the girl, Louise running behind him, one hand at her neck as if she were closing a robe. She rolled her eyes at Josie, who was not looking, transfixed instead by his suit, which seemed apart from his motion—containing his fat and possibly a million tiny broken veins such as the ones the afternoon sun caught in his eyes—a suit of herringbone and leg creases and grey pearl buttons to go with his eyes set too close together like "o's" in the word "look."

Then they were into the hall and Josie heard Louise push aside the chenille bedspread which hung over the entrance to the connecting hall. Beyond the curtain was the closed room. Josie imagined the peacock, whose tail feathers splayed the bedspread, had folded like an accordian.

"See what I mean!" Louise said.

In the hall leading to the one room they did not rent, Louise had stored her husband's goods—everything he had owned even though none of it was worth saving and so she had saved it all. It took up the whole hallway, stacked and piled, uneven shapes in the half-light from the dining room.

How did he die and what was Louise's reaction?

Consequent to a poker game, as the newspaper put it, and Louise, on seeing him and the color of his blood pouring from a hole a gun had made, tightened her muscles until they held and exploded. Her body had rocked, bones against themselves, hence her current layer of fat, against such a time in any future.

"It can't be helped," the landlord said. "I need to see to things," and he moved aside and went past Josie in the doorway and sat in a chair, filing his nails and waiting.

"Well for Christ's sake, help me," Louise said, and Josie, followed by the girl, put down her violin and began to carry boxes and suits and hunting gear out of the hallway and into the dining room. As they piled his things around the piano, the landlord watched and hardly moved, sweating in the heat of his still weight. Louise cursed, she said, "My back is killing me." When she looked at her watch, she said, "Oh my God," and scooted the girl out to her father. "Tell him we did theory," she called, "and never mind the money."

When everything he had owned was out in the bright light of the dining room, Louise pushed back her hair and said to the landlord, "Whatever it is, I hope it's worth it."

He got up from the chair and disappeared behind the door and didn't come out until it was almost dark. Louise and Josie were eating when he came back through. All the time he had been in the room, he had not made a sound, and now, Louise and Josie, tired from listening to nothing, had almost forgotten their own voices. The food tasted like nothing. Then, at the front door, he turned to say to Louise, looking at her without moving his head or his eyes, "My wife died in that room," and then their mouths tasted spit.

After he drove away, Louise sat beating on the table with a spoon. Josie, by herself, moved the belongings back to the hallway and pulled the bedspread straight again, the bird pastel in the muted light.

He came all summer and into fall, except that some Saturdays, he did not come, and the Saturdays he stayed away had no pattern to them. He did not say he was coming again or anything about when he would stop coming.

Louise thought each time was the last, and she put her husband's belongings back and pulled the curtain. Each time she moved them out again, she said to the landlord, "I can't do this much longer."

The girl who took violin lessons decided to stop taking the lessons, and Josie, having no job to do now that the girl was gone, put up her own violin and the sheet music by Mendelssohn.

Louise and Josie had little to say to each other about the landlord, about his wife. What they thought about, they thought about alone in bed.

Harry came home and Charlie stayed with him on Sundays and did not write any messages. But what Charlie did was expected, and even Harry, like an aftermath of himself, was not a surprise.

It was little things Josie noticed. The landlord's grey suit seemed each week to contain more cloth. And Louise covered her arms because she was losing her fat. They were growing thin together.

One Indian summer day, the landlord took off his suit coat and, once it was off, helped Louise move her husband's things to the dining room around the table. One night when Louise was hungry before she and Josie had a chance to move the things back to the hallway, they ate with his belongings there, and it seemed he had come to dinner.

The landlord always brought the valise, and both Louise and Josie noticed that, after a time, it began to look stuffed when he left. The first evening it seemed to Louise that he had something in the valise, she called to him from the couch, "So what did she die of?" because now his silence was like a quarrel between them.

"Of suffering," he said.

"My foot!" cried Louise. And he slammed the door as he left.

"I don't like him," said Josie.

"Like! Like!" Louise's voice had thinned with her body; it was one string.

Then, when even the landlord could see she was tired, the landlord consented one day to try to walk over and around the husband's things and get in without her moving them. And that evening, he stayed for dinner. Louise said such things as, "I get tired of all that driving around," and "There's just so much you can do with kids, and then that's it." And he said, "I can imagine," and "Not bad," of the food, and "I could help you move all that stuff out to the garage."

What sizes had the husband worn?

Coat: 42; shoes: 11½; socks: stretchable; shirt: 16½ tee-shirt: large; his favorite food was steak; he liked to sing but wasn't good at it; he loved

Louise and Josie; he never did discover why, exactly, he'd been born; and
when it ended, he had one minute in which to be surprised, and he used that
minute instead to notice the shape of Louise's hips, bones pointing inward,
as she ran up to him.

That night they moved everything to the garage, and when they had it all
arranged, Louise noticed that it had begun to rain, and she took one of her
husband's coats off a hanger and gave it to the landlord to wear, and he wore
it home.

With the hallway empty, Josie kept the light on, and, for the first time, she
looked through the keyhole of the locked door. In the morning light, what
she saw was bright, even with the shade drawn. Nothing left in the room at
all but a pair of shoes, blue and painted, with carved toes curved upward and
heels low, wooden, aligned on the wood floor, pointed toward a corner.

"Look!" she called, and when Louise came, they both tried to look at once,
and then they looked at each other.

After a time, Louise took Josie's room and Josie slept on the day bed. And
when the landlord came on Saturdays, Louise gave Josie money for the
movies, and when Josie came home, she found them talking in the living
room, and Josie went to look in her old room, at the pillow down at the foot of
the bed. The room smelled to her like all the weight they had lost.

When he went, he took the shoes, and he never came back.

Louise, some days, would wrap her arms around herself and, while
passing by a wall, run herself into it. She said one day, "Let's go see what
Florida is like."

They moved and they took all of the husband's belongings and stored them
in the new house Louise rented. She taught in a city school and didn't have to
drive far. Josie began to get the shape of a woman, and Louise grew fatter.
Only sometimes then did she run her body against a wall when passing by.
And Josie and Louise both had beds of their own, covered with spreads in the
pale shades of green and pink.

Charlie died, but only after Harry died. "Of *what?*" Louise wrote to
Charlie. But he didn't answer, and Louise dreamed once that Harry had died
while dancing, his feet of painted wood.

And Josie, who had never seen her father's body undressed in life or in
death, asked:

Would he ever come back?

Of course he would.

Litany (1)

My sisters, unlike me, don't keep themselves physically in shape. One away from the other is how their bodies slant. A piano chord loose from my thumbs, I look behind to see a chorus unglue their lips, think: they are joining at the hips, a Siamese-twin conclusion to being born.

If they claim our skin itself is bark peeling from The Cross, this I take to mean we are getting old. Our house does *not* resemble a prayer closet. "Gethsemane under the pines," says Claire, but I don't remember in The Original scrub brush, tin roof, shining even in the moon. The total effect careens.

No garden; the house stinks. Josie cooks at one end, we divert ourselves under bare bulbs at the other, go outside to pee and, there, watch the worms exit, find the open spaces in our toes.

Mother makes out like an angel. Claire and Josie ask, Why should *she* be stringent? Lizard-skinned, belly inching toward her backbone that much nearer-to-God, so, naturally, where else to put the money while we wait for a revival? In the trees over Father's '37 LaSalle out-of-gas (pictures of non-family girls in the trunk) Mom's garage house stirs with water, an 8,000 BTU conditioner for air, carpet red as flames for the ascent, daisies in a pot. I don't resent; I say quite simply, Old Dog, she never liked her nuns, her three bells. I myself leave her tray of food on the porch, with a note that says "God Knows" so the blood won't stop.

I don't tell Mother: We're still no holies. It's an assignment, no heart's glow—lovers falling in the grass. Work. *I* know what God said when the fruit

73

was gone, saliva on the detour out like banana peels. Nobody slept easy after except maybe Mary on whom I have dibs. *She* got told what was coming, down to the approximate sex. I exist on reading the signs, sniffing for rot, acquainting myself with wind subtle as what's carried in a bucket down a well.

Josie, nights, has begun to make the Charleston hammock sway under the trees like an invitation, regardless she says it's cooler, which I interrupt to ask, What about July when snakes fried on the tar. I look. Her long legs slip from the hinge, part and dangle on the sand. Some convict comes by, he might take her for a strip of moss imported from the Delta, sit on her, begin immediately sawing off the chains. She couldn't squeak though it's not his weight she'd want. I know she's been listening to Claire, preening for Father. I repeat: He's *not* coming.

Oh Josie, I grant you were so grand once. Married to a mechanic head-of-mechanics, running behind him from one concrete floor to another all across Charleston, taking his money to buy leather-bound books good enough for nameplates bearing your maiden name. Sterling silver forks and knives and spoons like we had, getting them engraved as you were accustomed before his name that unscrewed your tongue: Welborn. Waiting for cars to fall of the rack, I do not doubt, but he had instinct once he turned you over like a dog with a beetle. So he let you get frowsy-haired, as pacing includes innumerable visits to beauty parlors. Then he let you go. I pay him tribute, especially as you have read since him nearly all the books. I wouldn't say aloud: now he couldn't get you open.

But none of us is reading *Vogue* this month, despite we don't announce the party in preparation. I might go in and ask Josie, Who's going to eat those watermelon preserves? No. Discretion is the art of letting events flow downward, like water finding salt.

By me, Claire was seen yesterday among the pines, folding her fat down to gather drippings that will pass for rosin on the bow if the tune is for Pop. She reaches back 37 years and hums. Her hair's still fine; it glows. Why, she might, I think, even catch him if she doesn't turn around, except I'm practical, eye of the sphinx. I lean my head out the screen and call, "Play us a little worm music, will you?"

We eat dinner, Claire on the piano bench, plate on one end, her beside as in the old concert days before she taught me to play "Jesu, Joy of Man's Desiring" in her stead. "Mother sends her love," says Josie. "I accept," I answer, "pass the pâté can, that brand our dead father loved." They roll their eyes, they pretend this is a carnival during which any minute they'll go backstage and get The Slickest Man in the mid-west. I eat preserves, count the vitamin deficiency in every bite, abstinence and consumption in delicate balance in this body I keep fit.

Afterwards, cows we milk for money bellow from the neighbor's field; we sing. Claire goes up to hear Mother say her prayers, a thing I would not do since, last time, they were obscene, how she followed Father down every invention of the flesh, as if God and all the children didn't know. Like sand pouring through an egg-timer, it was. Amazing: she can remember every buckling under, every laugh when the appendages found what arrangements they could make.

Then, I go meet Richard for exterior contact and tell him, Bible or no in his overall pocket, I abstain, though for a cheek-kiss I'd take a little change, the tithe to keep Momma steady. He toes the dirt, he makes circles with his boot, and he says, "Explain that, will you, Lucy?" So I laugh girl-laugh and tell him, Never mind, let's walk a little. He's pure. His hair's the color of bantam roosters and his breath is hay. Sometimes I stretch my cause, I take his hand. "I love you, Lucy," he says.

Secretly, Richard, I tell the crickets who are loping home with me: I call you *Herbie* to myself, and I'd go so far as to eat with you moon-pie when it is time. Before this era, I also fell. He was nobody you could talk to eye-to-eye. Which I loved when the beginning's glued like adhesive on a sore. What do you *do*, Love? I never asked. I dreamed sheep-thief, child-catcher, pimp, and driver of cars which run against walls. His kiss fire, so full of disbelief at how I moved in time to nothing. Honey, the very bones untie. I wouldn't go down with you in any well-lit place.

Inside, I cut off the light hanging over my one-third of the pallet. If we had kerosene lamps, I could assure the olfactory sense. We are so impressed by sights; I defy anyone to see our panties drying in the sun and not think: flags. But never red. So I talk blood that smells, although to no one—Josie courting in a breeze no larger than mice-feet in the needles, and Claire still at her stichery: "Bless, bless, bless." What more can she *think* of?

"His lips," I say aloud, "were handsome, if at that moment encrusted. And that little pipe between them, it turned out to be the gear-shift—true. So I let them out of it by the gentlest pulling apart. You should have seen how nothing else was touched, and his eyes were the bluest blue, like sea when we go swimming nude. I swear I smelled salt mixed with the Gauloises on his tongue where bits of shredded tobacco stuck. He shirt was white, of course, but dotted at the last, I couldn't help it—his final wife, she was clawing at his face, at that smile we know enticed."

"I get so tired," says Claire, coming in to sleep, "of your particular prayers, and how you can't concentrate on anything that's real. It makes me want to sleep." Which she does, the gall of a former beauty imagining still that power, the refuge of knowing what you once were. I could only make me laugh by holding a mirror to her face. She is so sure, and now it is quiet as doves.

I think of mating games among the fish and fowl; I turn on the quilt afraid: being the only one to know he died is like if Richard suddenly turned himself in to me, walked naked in this room and said he was the same I talked to, how long can a man buy lollipops for a girl? And yet, tonight, I almost know what yesterday was sure. Lucy, you are fine, holding out so long when we all know what's known slips like glass through fire.

I dream in pairs: who tends the dove, who sends it out? There is so little entertainment here, so pitiful the exercise of flesh since we stopped the travels from Father and came here to imagine we are sitting down to tea.

We wake to grits, two months of grits, two months of buttermilk, and the rinds of pigs. Oh, when we were rich, we dined on quince, and ate from runcible spoons. I wipe the dream off, spy on plates of cake, and jams, and a solid ham cooling on a rack. Claire is such a stuffing, Josie yearns for Father's mouth to fill. "Pass a silver plate," I say, and, yawning, ask, "Who *is* coming out to tea?"

"You shit," they say in unison, "you *know*."

The food, it rots. And for a week, the rotting *smells*. On the second day, I feel my muscles jump; I go outside to think of Richard biting on my lips—I am so hungry with waiting. And the fools, they are polishing up their nails, making crimps in their bangs, after which I let loose my knots of auburn, shake my own red fist of hair in the sun.

When it gets cloudy, I recall a slight detail and, by the window, call up to Claire, "You coulda stole a choir robe, black or white; it didn't matter if there was nothing to wear when we were putting him away." She comes to the screen to blow dry a nail that's crimson against the whitest skin and fat. As it was, I had to go alone, then dragged the final wife along. Her stomach bulged and you could see *it* had nowhere else to go in order to begin with possible health. I made her sing a lullabye, then "Just As I Am."

Ritual, I think, is what keeps the stink away.

When there's nothing at all to eat, they take off to Pelzer to a fair. Josie's skirt is short; at any moment she might remember her high school days, jump up cheerleader-like and fall into a split. How old she is has gathered in the arms, up high where the bracelets fit tight as she saw in a magazine. They hold, in wrinkles, and her grin, it is no love of football players that makes a mouth eke, but truck drivers—what naturally follows mechanics, and one step short of fathers. I know.

Since I keep fit, I climb into a tree. The clouds are heavy as mothers of brides, but will dance in a month or two, heady with color, the shivering of leaves that brings the coldness on. I want a marriage bed of pine before the box: how to flush this family out?

I think: the women in town are wearing pink and yellow, and when they laugh, young boys hold up Japanese-made dolls on the ends of sticks, or on their hands. The ladies' teeth show gaps and stains. They want those dolls, off the sticks or on, and when they get the dolls, I know they'll want to trade them in for satin panties embroidered "Saturday" in lilac across the crotch. How their daughters will yell. Those greedy mothers, they'll end up taking both, go home and prop the doll up on a corner of the room where the man is waiting to see what creature came home from the fair, what bottled thing. She'll massage her own back, pretend, taunt him stiff as lace. They'll cover the house with love, and if he goes away, the territory itself expands. It can include states no one's seen. It is a wild, wild ride.

Herbie, I am afraid of laying down and the setting-to with eggs, since, afterwards, they hatch, then they come walking to watch and then they scrape you up. Like food, they lift you up. I sometimes dream: we could have gone as innocents; we could have ignored the cavil with the flesh.

They come home from the fair in a caravan of colors: I count white, white, flower-white, and choir-robe white, and the white of gauze. One car is orange under the moon and, under the porch light, her lips are orange too. They have found the last of Father's wives, and their baby cries in the car. Sliding down, I whisper, "Salome, his head will hang on the wall of your house forever."

Performance

She set the table for him, never forgetting the bread. She bought Gills Hotel Special coffee. She changed his sheets when she changed her own. And even: when he talked or moved, her body twitched, so much movement in the spine, the neck, the mouth, she didn't feel wasted.

They went on expeditions. In the stores, ladies selling material or lampshades thought of them as man and wife. But who cared in the country? She and her father had similar scavenger-hands and mobile lips, actor-like when the sellers hedged. He only bought at cost.

Now his house had a washer and dryer, a stainless steel sink. It had two velveteen cushions to go on the Danish chair, one cushion of yellow stripes, a motion-color; the other: brown flowers and brown leaves and black stems.

At one end of the L-shape, the house inside was paneled ash-gray, and at the other, chocolate brown. A black china bank in the shape of a pig sat on the window ledge in one room, to go with the ties which drew the curtains back. Yellow straw flowers were in the window where the sun hit first. His rooms more or less went together.

Here, she unbraided her hair. Time passed, and they waited for the electricity lines to make it down the road so he could hook up the machines and finish the house.

Four miles away, where the lines stopped, a seamstress sewed cushion covers, with welting and zippers and tassels. No plump couch to sit on and no unnatural light to read by, they slept a lot.

In the daytime, she embroidered. He envisioned one tapestry chair to sit beside the fireplace when it came time to unhinge the pots above the grate and put them on the Hotpoint. And he fingered the hems of the curtains she was to get to after the chair. What he saw were Chinese figures in a procession of legend. To her, they all looked alike: herself, her father, Chinese emperors, the Son and the Holy Ghost.

Their only relative who visited drove down from Tryon with a basketful of violet-colored plastic flowers, and bud vases with fluted tops, and revelations: "Christ's Disciples *married*. Finally. They got confused, of course. But *happy*. They married men."

"Which of your sisters *is* she?" she would ask him when Estelle drove off again, because he had two or three he hadn't mentioned enough for her to place.

"Shit. Get the whisk broom and get the hair off the back of the chair. And throw the junk away. *Bury* it."

It was long, red hair, hair that had never been cut, glorious hair left flowing around a wizened face.

"You didn't marry?" he asked her. (*He* had. "Yes, indeed, I did it twice.")
"No, no. I *might* marry," she said.
"Louise has the leaf to my dining room table, you know."

She should have married, but the oldest daughter and the youngest daughter had rushed, and once the succession was broken, it didn't matter when. She was *trying* to get ready. She wrote this man she might love secret letters, nothing in them: "The sun here is beautiful. I walk a lot—I had almost forgotten what it was like to be barefooted."

He would be amazed to see her like this, not very dressed. Only dressed when it was time to buy. He might not recognize her in wash dresses, her hair let down, the holes where the pierced earrings went dried shut. No makeup, a slight belly which might seem indecent to him unless it was seen after he made love to her, a shaking body loosed.

What sense she was after: being under him with not one thought available. *Then* she could talk in grocery stores. *Then* she wouldn't feel either naked in front of other people, the unsatisfied look always showing in tiny lines around the mouth, or too dressed, like a padding of fat, so anyone could wonder if she ever undressed all the way. How to like other women and the men who went with them and not on seeing think: house-play, and: I am ashamed.

He might ask, What are you *doing* down there? So she kept him quiet, like putting a wet finger on his lips, with these words about sand and the plumage of crows. Not very often; he wouldn't believe it very often.

So she was there for the summer routine. Her father taught it to her, and, if she forgot, he taught it to her again. Three times a week they ate eggs, two times a week oatmeal from Ireland because the grain was intact, one other morning nothing at all, to flush the system out, and on Sundays: anything they wanted.

There were six kinds of vitamin bottles, one much larger containing vitamin C, to put on the tiny table. He didn't want ridges forming on his gums, and he didn't want the walls of his arteries to lose their give. Meat for dinners, and always the salad, with no skins removed from the carrots, radishes, or tomatoes.

He looked her age. When she saw him for the first time in years, he said, "Well: why not?" *She* wanted to unroll, and then to stop flat.

He did get the newspaper, on Thursdays when the buys were announced and he could look from the back sections to his rooms and see what they had on sale he needed. Supposedly, the house would be done at once—a combustion, irreducibly complete when the last thing he wanted for it was advertised and slid from their hands to his hands and into place: the last variation finding its theme, or like a swan when the last feather's raised. And sometimes he forgot; he had her make notes. "A *watch*. A gold watch, not one of these Timex jobs. That ought to complete my jewelry needs."

Then, Fridays, they dressed. The kind of clothes to make a career in: cardigan jackets with silk blouses and gold-plated bracelets and virgin wool skirts and stacked heels and the limpest hose; or three-piece suits and shirts with cuffs and ties with matching handkerchiefs and hats of houndstooth plaids. He saw every stitch; they told each other when a button was loose. And they each liked how the other looked. In heels, she was his height. But he moved faster. He never paused.

She might write in a secret letter: "Love, we come home with big and little bags—thread or a mixer or three-quarter nails—and we dump them on the double bed in the room that's out of use, and we check them off the list, and all this time the sun is going down, flattening the sky, and is finally out except at the edges, like a plate—rimmed. I go look out the window, dressed like this (you would remember), and then, in this expanse, withstanding the twilight composed, I might be invincible. I might *promise*."

Except he would be afraid, as she was afraid of orchids, to read the extraneous.

"Look," her father said to a woman selling drapery at a department store. "I *know* there's been a man like me before who conceived of reversible drapes: this brown for the summer and this beige for the winter." And since the woman sent them both to the home office of the Armco stations where the woman thought she remembered seeing reversible drapes, it was very appropriate they were dressed like this, in the lounging area looking up at the tiny folds made in the German fashion with string. "Do you think you understand that?" he asked.

Finally the team from the electric company strung the house up. That night, they baked bread and broiled a steak. He got out the picture of Louise and put it on the wall where the inset light was. They didn't think to read.

"I might not want her back, you know," he said. "One night—we were living in Washington—she said to me, 'John, I've been thinking,' and I rolled my eyes and I said, 'Yes,' and she said, 'Maybe I haven't done the right thing.' So I had her call him up—ass—and she said, 'Could you at least go out when he comes?' and I said, 'If I'm out, I'm out, if I'm not, I'm in.' So he came and we moved the furniture over to his place."

"What about the little girl?"

"Well, sure, it was confusing to her. Louise would come over and bring her and she'd run up and say, 'Daddy, do you love us?' and I'd say, 'Sure, honey, but your mother can't make up her mind what she wants.'"

"She's pretty. They're both very pretty. Mother was pretty too."

"Your mother talked too God-damn much."

The morning after the electricity lines had been attached, he took out his Skil saw, to even the beams which stuck out irregularly from the tin roof. She got her little sewing machine from her car and put it on the table, and soon there was a double hum, inside and out, his long drone and her short rasps as she tried to remember how to make the drapes with a string hidden inside. She could see his legs from where she sat, or, rather, his jeans of the heavy 16-ounce denim which stayed still in the absence of a breeze, only lifting slightly when he moved across the scaffold. Then she looked up later and saw he must have moved.

But he was at the door; he said, "O.K." through the screen, and when he opened it, she saw first how white his face was, then how red and dripping the handkerchief was wound around his hand.

"What you do—listen carefully—is go out and look for it. I've cut a thumb off, and I want it sewn back on, and while I drive to the doctor's you have to find it, you have to wrap it in ice, and bring it over to the doctor's at the corner near Frank's. Do you have that?" His teeth were barely moving, his jaw twitched. But, otherwise, she could see: it was a *job*.

"Wrap it tight," he said, and after she had put a t-shirt around the handkerchief and tied it with string, he said, "Now you do exactly what I said."

But even in the sun, she couldn't find the piece of his hand in the sawdust and shavings. She got sick looking, especially sick when she realized he hadn't cried out. And besides, they had not remembered to connect the refrigerator, and the ice in the chest was gone. It was done. She walked to the spring at the edge of his property and stuck her own fingers in the cold water.

And he saw it was done, too. When he came back bandaged at dusk—a wasted day—he said, "All right. It was my fault. But I hate it. I hate it."

With his hand useless for construction, he went off for two weeks to do piece work with his typewriter, the hunt and peck system, writing speeches for politicians who needed dedicative oratory for libraries and county fairs. He had connections; the jobs had beginnings and ends and no one remembered him unless he came around again.

In his absence, she sewed. She pretended to be away when Estelle came the first Saturday, banging on the door and calling out, "Johnny! Oh Johnny, are you home?" Then, back a dozen paces from the door, among the first row of bushes, she squatted and, in tongue, blessed the house, or cursed it, or simply received a sign.

It rained, and sometimes lightning accompanied the rain, so she stopped sewing. She sat cross-legged on the twin bed, flinching with the light and the roll of thunder. He seemed to be missing—the way he lived. A stylist. And she counted her own practical talents. Really, she thought, they must be separate—the sewing and cleaning and rocking—or: what is the point, bedding down? She might write: I *want* to be faithful. Except what she meant was no lover's concern.

She felt sleepy when he got back, and ashamed of how little work she had done to pay for her meals and bed and the quiet. He brought the couch covers back with him, and when she got the foam stuffed in, they took turns flopping down. For whatever reason, the covers were bright red and the welting gray and the loose cushions brown. But it was a very soft couch. He slept there the first night, and when she got up to make breakfast, she saw the bandage was off, and the wound rounded with skin.

First, the table-leaf came by postal express, in a narrow crate, so on the expanse of the table, he put new candles.

"Did she write?"

"I gave her ten dollars for her trouble, if that's what you mean," he said. "Besides, we're satisfied, aren't we?"

"I thought . . . ."

"Don't think," he said laughing. "Eat up."

Then Estelle's two boys drove down. They thought Estelle was the one coming, the sound of her pickup on the ruts in the road, and them parking in the same place she parked, at the edge of the creek he hadn't bothered to bridge, it was so shallow and only bothered her.

The boys walked up saying, "God! Some crazy pad!" and let the screen door slam behind them. Her father came out dressed for them, in a wool serape and a turtle-neck shirt and corduroy pants. But Raymond and Jesse didn't seem to notice, to appreciate. They went around picking up the red glass rooster on the mantle and the bottle in the shape of a violin and the brass tray, whistling between their lips, and when they got tired, they started strumming on the red-painted guitars they carried with them. "Uncle Johnny, what'll it be?"

"Your preference, boys," he said; then, "No, I know—play a little Dylan. I heard the kids went wild over him. Let's hear what for."

Raymond flipped the hair off his forehead and picked out a tune, talking while he played, first the words to the song, then, "You heard the *kids* liked it, huh? You think maybe it wasn't your sweet little bride? and oh, how the times, they is all blowin'. . . ."

Jesse, the little polite one, said, "Serious, where'd you get all this stuff?"

"More to the point," said Raymond, "is when do you *work*. Work?"

She was stiff, and, suddenly, she liked *Estelle*. But he wasn't mad, he sat tapping his feet.

"Tell you what, boys," he said. "I'll take you on a little ride, I'll show you a little bit of Americana. I'll—no, look at it this way: which of you does what? Jesse?"

"Work on the line, down at Fork Shoals."

"Raymond?"

"Truck-driving-man. Why you say?"

He wouldn't wait for her to dress, so she went in the same dress, and sat up front in the Hudson next to him, the boys in back, snickering and punching each other in the ribs until he pulled over to the side of the road and asked, "Well, do you or don't you: want to learn something? Make up your minds."

"We do," they said, "we do."

When they got to I-75, he pulled off the median and made them all get out and start collecting all the bottles along the strip. He opened the trunk and told the boys to put them there. It was getting dark; cars were infrequent, but when one came by he stopped, and with the bottles stuck on his fingers, nine where there might have been ten, he watched the car go by, and it was a flapping silhouette, with color from the bottles and the yellow flash of the headlights. Little Jesse inched the car forward so they wouldn't have to walk so far. And in an hour, they had the trunk full and the car floor full, and Jesse and Raymond had to sit with their feet on the bottles while he drove to the A and P to cash them in.

"All right!" her father said. He counted out five dollars to Jesse and five dollars to Raymond and one-fifty for the glove compartment. "That's what I mean to tell you," he said. "Americans waste. And if you learn that simple basic principle, you're on your way."

In the lights of the parking lot, the boys folded their money and shuffled their feet, solemn, and when they got back to the creek, they jumped out, and Jesse went in to get their guitars, and they said, "Bye," and they drove off without wheelspins or headlights to scare the rabbits stiff in the road.

She ached.

Then a time of good weather came, and the house was noisy with banging and sawing and boards bumping and wrenches knocking on pipes and him splashing his feet in Epsom salts. Every day or so he looked around and said, "Well!" It grew hotter, and she tied his work shirts around her like a halter. They went out buying less, using what he had, rushing because the heat was oppressive and because it was the last summer month.

She had no idea how to make the figures on the curtain hems. She used a bit of black thread and white dots for cheeks on what looked a little like women's faces, and many sprays of cherry blossoms. She sat with the material across her lap, on the cool stone steps, lifting the material now and then to let a breeze hit where she sweated between the knees. The steps faced the road, far off and almost moving, the light playing tricks, and she knew that if she walked to the mailbox, black snakes would be asleep on the tar.

From where she sat, he was a shadow, and the ladder was another shadow, and the scaffolding another. Around her feet, the extension cord for the saw moved as he moved. She looked up at the road and down at the thread and sometimes to the shadows, as if *they* were working and were not a semblance. And then: he fell.

She saw the fall in this semblance, a flash across the ground, and then the sound from around the corner, and the sound of the cord jerking from the outlet inside the house. But she wouldn't move. No.

It was Estelle who made the procession come—all the children and their children and their children's children, and even Louise and the little girl, and even the Senator from their district who gave a speech he wrote himself, and even the oldest and the youngest daughters. Cars of all colors strung around the hills and down to the house, and the screen door slammed open and shut. And he looked almost the same, the broken parts covered with a paisley quilt they had bought together at J. M. Field's, the head a little raised on the newly covered couch where they put him, Estelle and the boys, and the partial thumb covered with the other fingers, her part. It was a busy wake.

Except for Estelle and Raymond and Jesse, none of them had seen the house. And, with him gone, it looked a mess.

They took her, them coming in pairs and alone, into the corners of the house that day. And they whispered, over and over, "You were here with him: What was he trying to *do?*" But she shook her head.

Why talk?

Light

It will seem no time has passed when Ann gets up from the floor and walks through the doorway filled with light.

Light which was meant first for her mother.

Norma lies at this time on a day bed and covers herself to her chin with a sheet. "Hot," she says, a pronouncement, as in deaths.

One day her skin will show through the sheet when the door opens. It will appear blue, her body as one long vein. Her breath will catch—Ann will remember breath itself can seem to break, and the sound of her dress brushing at the doorway will mend this sound. And later, in Ann's own breath, as if the voice carried blood faces of red and white, will be the face of her mother.

And Ann's dress will be off-white, it will appear golden, as if (when the time had come and Ann wrapped Norma in the burial dress and tucked it close so that her hips took on the shape of a lily curling into its green spike) she had not broken when, in fact, she broke and held herself together with light. Never so naked. This is a wedding tour, a cacophony of preparations leading to the dance.

"Won't it ever cool off?" cries Norma from the day bed. "And where is your father anyway?"

Naming Ann's attendants: fever, loss.

Norma would be a silly woman but for the way she turns her body inside out. *Trousseau.* Originally? *A bundle.*

Outside there is a sidewalk three feet from the door and so, always, they keep the curtains drawn. Across the sidewalk and the grass is an identical row of apartments. In the back are garbage cans and clotheslines. Everywhere there is sun—this is Ventura, California, on a straight shot to L.A.

"Look at this," says Norma. And she throws off her sheet to show Ann her sunburned skin, appendages blooming, between her legs a black cluster of seeds. Then she drops the sheet like a parachute, sinks, begins to snore in dream-waters.

Fever.

But Ann has her devices—ten years of memory on the head of a pin where another's faith would go. This time, elongated fingernails of Chinamen dealing in Rice Crispies at the local Sun Mart. She is actually cold, placing these men very gently back among the mountains she thinks they came from, the Himalayas. In her hands is a bride doll who sleeps; cool air, cold light.

In the evenings when her father comes home from what is his work, he takes her for walks which seem long. At the corner of their street, they stand looking in the twilight at the road which runs to Los Angeles. Because she has never seen the town and because she cannot see it now, here on the sidewalk, what is mysterious fits her father's palm, enclosed by their fingers. Of course he loves her.

This day, he is in the foyer of a studio, waiting to move into a film. He has handed over his card, taken the orange chair, crossed one leg and lighted a cigarette. One day he will have a photograph taken in this pose—the chair will be brown velveteen—because (he *must know*) it is impossible when his body is arranged in such a fashion to conceive why he did not make it in the movies.

He waits all day. The body never slips, even as Norma sinks downward into seaweed.

At the end of the day he walks out as if he didn't remember: one leg is two inches shorter than the other leg, one shoe is two sizes smaller than the other shoe. Walks as if: "Who gives a shit?" in the era, yet, of Victor Mature laying on hands. Ann's father's bright teeth flashing. . . . Norma opens her mouth in sleep. And then it is twilight.

"Make her get dressed."

"Make her eat, then."

Ann whispers. The rooms are dark as a movie house.

"Does she eat any lunch? Here, with you? *You* eat." All questions—Ann is so small in her sundress, its lace aflutter on her arms.

She and her father sit across from each other at the formica-topped table and share a can of sardines and a package of crackers. Inside both scatterings of crumbs is a spoon; between them a cut cantaloupe. In the living room there is only the day bed, Norma, a small table where Ann's doll sleeps.

"No. She doesn't eat anything! Not hardly anything at all!" Her voice rising, eyes widening.

Back goes the chair, scraping on the tile floor. Up, the navy blue suit with pin stripes. The voice a trail of breath: "I'll make her eat. By God, *eat.*" Norma, her sheet: held up against the wall as if she had no weight. *"Eat."* Her red back scraping the plastered walls. Her scream. And he throws her down.

"I can't make her eat."

For Ann's walk, he lifts Ann from her chair and carries her to the yard and swings her around, he dips her feet in a child's wading pool, and then he lets her go. She squeals, he pretends to be Harpo Marx, and, for a long time, they refuse to talk to each other.

On the grass by the road leading toward town, he asks her, "Remember the watch?"

Ann thinks this watch is hidden somewhere on Harpo, in the pockets of his huge eyes, so she rolls over to where her father is resting on the grass and she presses his eyes shut seven times and wrinkles her nose.

"No, silly," he says. He tousles her hair. *"This* watch." He taps his Bulova. "Now listen carefully."

She settles back in the grass beside him, placing one arm beneath her head the way he has done. Seen from high up, she is exactly half his height. They listen to the grass settle.

"Well?"

"Well? Well, it was this way. You should remember. Try to remember while I tell you."

"I remember."

"You do not. Listen. Learn." He clears his throat; there is no trace of the South left in his voice. "We were driving out here for the first time. We had two cars then. Your mother drove one, I drove one, and you rode with me because we had all the house-things in the Nash. It had seat covers, mine didn't."

"Still doesn't." Ann turns to look at him.

"Hush. Now: crossing the Mojave is no small trick. We tied thermos bags on the radiators, I bought you a basin and filled it with water so you could sit in it and be cooler. Your mother, as I recall, took off her blouse and drove in her bra. She would. And we started out. Both cars gassed up full. And we did fine—no sand storms, no flats. Of course when we got to the other side we drove in to the first service station and stood around inside and rested. That's when I noticed my watch was gone. Remember?''

''No.''

''Well of course we had to go back and get it. Your mother said, 'Ridiculous,' but we turned around and set out. I knew we'd find it—a Bulova, you know.''

''Let's see again,'' Ann asks, and he holds up his arm.

''Gold,'' he says.

She nods. ''So how'd you find it?''

''You, of course! I remembered the last time we stopped was to let you pee. So I looked for a little dark spot by the side of the road. You would think the sun would have dried it out. But no, there it was. And right by it, my watch, because I'd helped you unhook your sunsuit.'' He turns to Ann. ''See there? How it is?''

''Me,'' she answers. Then they don't talk, they listen to the cars passing.

Ann rolls over in the grass closer to him. ''I know something,'' she says. ''Something *I* remember. Right before we set out, we stopped at a restaurant and had steak. A whole, huge steak each. This man behind the counter cut mine into little pieces so I wouldn't choke.''

''*He* cut it?''

''Yes, like this.'' Ann makes a whittling motion with her hands. ''Fast. Every piece was about so-tiny.'' She holds up her right thumb and first finger for him to see.

Looking, her father asks, ''Why didn't I cut it?''

''You were thinking. I remember.''

''Ah. So I was.''

Then it is time to sleep.

Norma rises in the middle of the night. She gets a towel from the bathroom, wets it, wraps it across her shoulders and around her neck. She goes to stand at the doorway of the bedroom where Ann and Rhett sleep. Two narrow beds. Behind the closet door: all his clothes. The shirts of camera-blue.

He grits his teeth in sleep, and Ann, in the light which filters through the white shade, is beautiful.

She raises herself, one day, on one arm, and looks down at Ann cutting from a magazine white dresses for her doll. Norma says, ''Now get this.'' She waits.

Ann looks up, the scissors held in mid-air, open and hot. "Yes, Momma?"
"Before you were born, I was a beautiful woman."

Ann's recurring dream is in a field close enough to the shore that sand still makes a light cover where brush takes root. Ann lies in the curve of two rises and lifts her head—a woman's head on the body of a baby—and chews off her connecting cord. Sunlight; a triumph; she crawls away. Off the edge of the dream, she stands.

Years later, Norma is watching television on a pink, nubby couch. She smokes and fingers the arm of the couch. On the screen is a bulletin, no picture, a voice: the wife of a famous man has, twelve hours after giving birth, lost one of her twins, a boy. The lungs refused to inflate; they filled with water. And Norma sucks in her breath and holds it until her face is scarlet, an explosion in miniature.

Ann, although she is sixteen, slips from the couch to the floor and cries, "I knew it. I knew it. I knew it."

And suddenly she is in love. She lies on the floor, holding her belly, her voice inside a miniature madness: *My brother, unlike me, didn't keep himself in shape. His body apart from my body was how his body grew.*

Norma snaps off the television with the button of the remote control. Her legs are pocked with holes; she no longer pursues her career of selling Cora jewelry. She looks at Ann, her eyes don't move, they say, It is true. And Ann's recurring dream takes on its own shape.

Ann's father drives her by a low, small building. It is October; they have forgotten school and on this day he remembers. "That's where you went to kindergarten," he tells Ann, pointing to a room whose windows are decorated with black cats and orange pumpkins. "Remember?"

"I don't think so."

"Of course you remember!"

Ann slips down in the Packard car seat and tries to think. "Five. What was I like when I was five?"

Her father has directions to the new school written on a piece of paper beside him. He studies the paper. He smiles. "Well, Sugar," he says, "just like now."

"Really?"

"Well sure." He rubs her head. He shows her the new school, the route from where they live, and, so that she will have something to take to school when she goes in the morning, he buys her a book called *The Twenty-Four Ivans*.

In the evening after their walk, Ann reads on the day bed beside Norma of the men who were so incredible they slept with their legs tied to logs floating in a river. In sleep their heads slipped into the water and when they woke, they pounded their chests and said 24 times, *"Marvelous!"*

At supper one night, Ann's father asks, "When does she eat?" He taps his spoon on the table. "No. What I mean is, when does she go out in the *sun*. *That's* what I want to know."

"Me?" Ann asks.

"Who else?"

"I don't know, I'm in school."

He says, to anyone, "She's red. Red! She's *crazy!*"

Ann leans over close to him. "Poppa? In school, I cry."

"You do?" he asks. "Well stop it." He gets up from the table and goes to look down at Norma. Her eyes are red, as if she has been crying, which can't be. He kicks the metal frame of the day bed. "Bitch," one long breath.

Norma kisses Ann one morning as Ann leans down, her braids brushing on Norma's chest, a tickle of ribbon. "Ann?"

"Yes?"

"When you feel sorry for yourself, remember the Mexican children out there. You know what they eat? *Paste*. School-paste. Whole big jars of it. They steal it and eat it. And the Chinese around here? Rice. White rice. Nothing but white rice. I heard about it."

On Halloween, it is still hot. "Here it is always hot," says Norma. "Here it never cools off." Ann doesn't know how to trick or treat in such heat, what costume, because the colors from the one Rhett has bought for her bleed on her hands in such heat.

"Will you take me around?" Ann asks her father, because she imagines ghosts of all-white, fat or thin.

"No," he answers. "I'm too big. Your mother should go. But she won't."

"I won't," says Norma.

Ann dresses herself in her bathing suit and, to be specially dressed, stuffs handkerchiefs in the top so that she is as big as Norma. She wears Norma's mascara and her rouge, the magenta lipstick. Down comes her long hair. Someone seems to whistle at her when she is in the bathroom, but when she turns around, no one is there.

From the row of apartments, she gets in her bag five Baby Ruths, two Sugar Daddies, three packages of Dentine gum, a ball of popcorn tied with red cellophane, five pennies, apples and oranges and little boxes of raisins such as she has never seen before. She is barefooted, her feet burn.

At one apartment, two boys who are as tall as men answer the door. Behind the screen they look at her together. She begins to hold out her sack, but the men elbow each other in the ribs, which show because they are dressed, as she is, in their bathing suits. One laughs, he says to his friend, "She'll get hers." He opens the screen door and lets out a thin, blue aura of light from the television. "Oh, don't worry," he says. "You will get yours." They laugh as Ann runs.

Is this what Norma has? The body aflame?

In time, Ann and Norma will move. They will travel from place to place among relations who remember them vaguely because California exists for some people and never for others. These relatives keep cows and want to know where "he" is.

"Here comes The Bad Penny!" cries Norma each time she drives up for visits. They smile, they take Ann and Norma in—an assortment of men unlike Ann's father, and their women: shadows who serve oatmeal in bowls with handles, brown sugar on top. It makes the stomach burn.

"Too late," white-suited men will say of Norma's body, pointing to the red marks on her legs, which grow like flowers, die, sink in, harden like black pearls.

One morning Ann's father takes her aside. He has cleared his closet; on one side Ann's pinafores flutter as he slides the door shut. Outside, at the end of the apartments, sits a car which is almost tangerine-colored and, but for that color, like the car Norma drove to California when Ann was five: Ann remembers. Her father walks around it, kicking the tires.

"It'll do," he says. He turns to Ann. "You ride in the back—at all times—you understand?"

She nods her head, because of his voice—a bone rattling among bones.

"In case," he tells her. "In case . . . ," he says to himself because, Ann can see, he is not present. *Thinking.*

The day passes. They all sit together. No one eats, or thinks of eating. And Norma looks, but at what?

"I want to go outside," she says. A request.

"No."

In this time, years pass. Ann flowers in white, only her lips Norma's singular color, a gift as another might give sterling or Wedgewood.

In the manner in which she has learned not to cry, Ann learns how to walk loose-hipped. Men look. Some imagine she is a door, behind her: everything. They say, after a time, "You're crazy, you know it?" Quietly. Leaving as if they were drawing a shade, the disease both light and dark. They are afraid. *Of what?*

Often Ann agrees, as if she knew what she were agreeing to. It is an old, old habit, the oldest thing she owns. She wears it: "Yes," her own breath at this time broken.

At sunset, Rhett makes a speech, as if he were before a camera. He is dressed in navy blue; one leg is crossed over the other leg; he lights a cigarette. This is a cameo.

"Listen carefully," he says. "I'm going. I won't be back. Norma, I've bought you a car. Ann, your mother will drive you back to Pelzer. She *will*, in time she will, because, you see, you have to grow up, and your mother knows it." He looks to Norma's location. "She knows it." And, turning to Ann, "I promise that. Now: this is for you. This isn't for your mother. Come here."

Ann gets up and moves to his chair. He holds her, his arm a small circle. "Learn not to cry," he says. "Maybe not right now. But learn not to cry. You won't last long if you cry. I've learned that. Promise me?"

"Oh, I promise!"

The door opens, he is gone, a brilliant shaft of light comes in the room. The screen catches and doesn't shut. They wait for it to close, then Norma begins to laugh.

Slowly, in the time in which the screen door would have shut, Norma, coverless, begins to arch her hips, up and down in a rhythm which Ann knows in the instant she turns and watches.

Ann runs to Norma and covers her with the sheet. Norma's body, as her breath catches, is one blue vein.

Now, in present time, Ann goes through a doorway. Her dress is golden. In her breath, as if the voice carried blood faces of red and white, is the face of her mother.

"Wait," he calls to her.

You are not crazy, he had said. "You are not crazy," he says.

And Ann turns, and is running, he and she are laughing. In the bus loading zone, he lifts her up and they swing around and around: both laughing. In such a place.

Under the canopy, passengers look the other way, as if they were ashamed of such voices and bodies.

But Ann cannot see them; she is in sunlight.

My Brother, Unlike Me

Packing, unpacking. We did a lot of that in those days, suffusing the goods with dreams, lies. No more, I guess, than other families also bound for California or Washington State where red apples fell so lightly you could open your mouth under a tree and not get bruised. Sweet pain! They wanted some of that, my family in my father's lead. All but me.

I packed first, my little bundle under a tree, the violin bow making it mysteriously long. I wouldn't for anything have had them know I wanted to play.

What *did* California have to do with fingers pressing the right spaces and rosin smoothing out the notes?

My father knew. The way he moved said: I know everything. He knew people you had to call by first and last names together. No "mister," and, as for the women he knew, my mother called them all "Her," and he said he didn't know who she was talking about.

Air-tight reason: I learned from him.

He said to Mother, "Jay Rosenfeld said the last time I called him . . . ." And you knew Jay was God Himself in Spring.

Well, Papa, I am *here* in the greenest Spring, educated past my wildest dreams.

He called up once, saying, "Hello, this is Jim Rhodes speaking." I put the receiver down softly. Stranger!

So they were in a commotion of lies the Depression Follow-up had made, half of what we owned on the dirt yard and half still in the house, with him going in and out because, he told Mother, everything "down to the last sombitch piece" was going into that trailer.

My older sister rolled her eyes, trying to mesh hers with mine. *No*, Sweet Alice.

My mother said to Jim Rhodes she knew we'd be back, so why not leave the stuff that was easiest to leave. "We *always* end up here!" she said, rue in her voice, spit like pollen.

Mother didn't know how far California was. She thought the trip would be like other trips, flick, flick. Time like a fly across your face is what she thought, and, unless you were dead, it didn't light.

I walked off down the road. Waiting, and why not gather him up some cigarette butts too. Anne, she would be getting out her little quilt bag where she hoarded hard candies and be selling some to Sweet Alice for a lot of pennies, even though under the threat of death. Sweet Alice was the devil himself. When my father limped, she was taller than him. I could never mention his one short leg. *He* knew.

Half the times there was nothing in the mail box. Once, a little green snake. Others, my mother would start taking me on walks past the creek and past the milk-lady. It might be October. She would say, "Don't forget your times-tables. You'll need them soon. Have you forgotten them?"

"No."

But it was accidental. For instance, there were five of us—him, her, and us three girls. But he called us girls "Joleen" or "Ester" or "Lois" or "Irene" and sometimes "Margaret-Lee" after a sister of his we never got to see. The others, like sisters of his might, resembled him but when you saw them, you never forgot them. They let their hair go wild. And they were big as him, not having been touched by polio. They wore reds, all shades; they looked crazy in the eyes. (We all had intelligence.) With us girls getting their names when he forgot, and Jimmy, ours, the boy who had died early, looking like me, and photographs of others of the Rhodes in the house on the walls, and them sleeping in Grandfather's bed where we had *seen* him die, we were more than five. How much more remained a questionable number.

"Would you like to go off somewhere?" Mother would ask. She would wait. "Without *him*," she would finally say, nodding her head back toward the little rise.

He would *kill* me. "I don't know. Where, like?"

"Oh, I don't know," she would say. "Someplace nice. Maybe get a goat. I always wanted a goat. Goat's milk. It's good for your skin. You take care of your skin."

We would pick blackberries, go home, make him a pie even if he had decided not to remember us, and give him the butts so he could roll some cigarettes.

Then, after some days, she would get a letter. She would wash up, and wait.

More than once he bore those flotillas of elegance coming as if out of the sky down the road and into our roadway—black Packards and shiny DeSotos. Her friends out of a past which had held the inheritance and, still, the manners she could pick up off the table like a pair of gloves.

We each got a quarter pressed in our hands when she turned at the door. "Be decent."

They never came in, these men who must have belonged to her old school friends. Everybody was married. I slept in one of their houses once. Green walls, white woodwork, a clock over the refrigerator. "I don't remember that," Mother would say. "I don't think we did that. Did we?"

You could see the high-yellow of night coming down when they drove off—too late to spend the quarter, and *he* wouldn't move. He would sit with a little smile. He would wait.

I couldn't find the letters. Maybe he had them. Then, a sister of his would come and cook for us a while—the one who didn't wear underclothes.

When Mother got back, we ate the borrowed money up. He made gourmets of us all. Eat good or nothing. It makes the stomach touchy. Gets to where it responds.

Then, us all fatter on artichokes and drawn butter, he would get her back. Fat like a mammy and having been looked at like mammies are when they go to church with the red slip on and it showing—he would let her come down from it, starve a little, and then he would tell her he wanted to go to "Orlando, Florida."

"Where *is* that?"

He would get out Grandfather's truck and drive it over to Pickens and fill it up out of Grandmother's garden, and he'd get the Hurlburt Bibles out of her chiffonier, and he would stay gone a day or so, selling. Bring her a new pack of Camels and pinch her fanny and roll her on the bed.

"California," he would say.

"Get off a me."

But, he was, in many ways, as handsome a man as you would ever want to meet, and when he did fail as an extra in California, nobody ever said it was because one leg was short.

Rebba, the oldest sister of his (with the most eye-lines like his, to rule out the possibility the crinkles came from laughing when it was really a blood-characteristic) had a saying. She would look over the little living room strewn with his publicity pictures from a lot of enterprises, and a few Navaho blankets and a vase of orange and red on the mantle, and the tape recorder and a few sets of silver cuff links here and there. She would say, "I don't know where he gits it."

True.

But Mother had a theory: He learned what he knew in the Shriner's Hospital in Asheville, North Carolina between the ages of five and seven and a half. The nurses and the doctors and the simple mechanics of medicine— cleaner than any earthly thing.

"Nobody *dies?*" we three would ask her.

"Well, sure, they die. *Some*times. But what I mean is . . . I don't want to talk about it."

It made death pure. Anybody might rise.

In California and in little towns as near to California as you can get without getting over the line, we grew up. I grew up. Waist and hips and my own little flotillas of elegance which would stand me in good stead when it was my time for men to come get me in big cars. Mother gave everything a sequence, one revelation following another.

Sweet Alice went mad after we left Jim Rhodes—lost him in, I believe, Orlando. She bloated up, a puffa-fish, and then, in *her* time, she came down again, and began a career—music, as the rhythms were inbred and could flow out her fingers. If he could see her now!

When I got back with the Durham bag filled, Mother was surrounded with her Wedgwood china. Wrapping, unwrapping. He rolled a cigarette and watched. Her hair was drawn back in a rag, her legs spread wide in front of her, a little gravy bowl between them. "They will *break.*"

"I got you the best packing material they had."

"You'll end up pawning them, then. Remember the clock?"

"Not this time, Sweetie," he said, "so don't take all day."

It was twilight already, but what was time to him but money? She looked around to see where we all were. "Go do something," she said. "Don't just look." She bit her lower lip as if she might cry, might break out and touch one of us. She never did; she was against it.

Sweet Alice rolled her mouthful of red hot cinnamon balls and said, "I'll do your hair." Mine that was lovely.

He came out on the porch when she had the lather on me. Soap was on the table, and her big rollers and some little rods to make crimps. "Women," he said. He looked through the screen at Mother folding up some linens. He slapped a Max Brand western on his thigh.

Sweet Alice said, "Shit," when he left, and threw a towel at me. "Do it your own self. It's a waste."

Anne was asleep, holding on to her quilt bag, one thumb in her mouth: her, the last of us, the one who might open up a business of her own and get rich, which she did, and married a lawyer so that everything she ended up owning was in one place.

Behind the trailer, a moon was hoisting itself up, and the dog chased a rabbit in the woods. Mother sighed to us all, a loud stage sigh nobody believed anymore, would not believe until it turned out that Father was all she got—couldn't, in the future, move herself enough for another man, and, like Anne, put everything down in one spot. Not so big a place, not even, in fact, adequate, and got a mean dog to protect it when the times turned and made thieves of mavericks. She loved Father for his purity, it turned out.

I walked toward the back of Grandfather's property, to his burial place and the site pegged for Grandmother on his right and next to Little Jimmy's— plots consecrated by a few neighbors' deaths which made, with foreign bones, the ground legal. All but these neighbors were shaped like me, his side, my life-long project being to grow-in-grace more like myself, even if the bones give.

Mother had a theory about Little Jimmy. It went: if he hadn't died, if Jim Rhodes had had a son he could count on, then he might have been a farmer like his father planned, and settled, and passed something on.

When I got back to the house, they were all asleep—Mother where she had been, in a pile of old blankets, her beauty on a wane you could almost touch. I slept and half-slept on the stone steps, arms gathered around the rib cage, holding in, a backlog on a fire.

The next morning, Mother wrapped and Father packed. In the front bedroom, he lit a cigar. When she walked past him where he was laying out a suit to drive in, she sniffed and said, "Silly." He slapped her; we each heard it.

She walked outside and, in a high sun, began to cry. We, all but him, gathered around her—the new sound, a low, rummy sound. I saw how large her rib cage was. She was taller than I thought, she had feet like Sweet Alice and Anne's fat nose.

He came out dressed and stood at the screen door watching her, one hand at his bow tie. "You'll like it," he said, "you'll see."

We all moved away, decent listening distance, her cries coming loud and soft as she put things in a box, then brought her head out again. My sisters thought she had stopped; they drifted off. Father helped her sort. He went in and out of the house, bringing things to hold up at the screen door. He asked, "Winter or Summer—what do you think?"

Mother wrapped up his brandy glasses and the wine glasses, holding each one up, looking through before wrapping it up. She hadn't combed her hair. Over beside her was her bowl of cereal, blue-green flies on the rim.

When Father came out carrying stacks of photographs and set them next to her, light coming off the glass, she said, "Can't we leave just those, like a part of the house?"

He winked at her. "You will, you'll *like* it!" He turned to me. "Right?" he asked. He said to Mother, "Rebba knows." Meaning me.

The long, laid-low answer: She didn't like it.

And: It didn't last.

And the sun ruined her skin.

She began to whimper, jerking her head up, her lips loosening. She turned to me. "We aren't going to leave a thing!" Voice up, wild at the end.

I stooped down by her and I said in a whisper, "You forgot Little Jimmy. He stays. I mean it's something."

She looked at me for a long time, her face changing while I waited, all her history passing by, her times-of-times. Then she hugged me.

Why?

As it turned out, we didn't get back to Grandfather's farm. Through the California years, she surprised me—she hugged me, passing by now and then. I might be reading in a chair, forgetful. Then she herself forgot.

We left Father in one of those towns, and when he moved on too, he didn't leave a forwarding address. There were a lot of stars who made it, doing what must have been a much worse job.

I grew up.

I began to fall in love with a particular kind of man, again and again, as the rhythms are inbred and I was never good with the violin.

Oh Little Brother, the shame of it when I think of it, paste in my joints: You didn't keep yourself physically in shape.

Lovers

Juanita keeps her hair clean, as if she were scrupulous. And there are life-stories she would not have as her own, now or ever. She cuts them from newspapers, saves them until someone visits, reads them aloud and shudders. Juanita.

Named so long ago by another mother so long dead, it would be pointless to tell how she got this name suggestive of castanets and lace. Before long, a minister may officiate at rites for Juanita, click his false teeth in a rhythm—ashes, dust. Someone may, beforehand, dress her in lace, see in the coffin an incredible flirting.

Her hair is so clean it lifts in any breeze—a refrigerator door closing—and shows her white scalp. When she sits, the red dress stretches across her knees. Juanita's daughter Cynthia, goddess of the moon, watches Juanita spread her legs, or, rather, the leg muscles go slack. Cynthia sees Juanita does not wear underclothes. Sees the blue-grey body hair, and is sick.

Across the road is a new home for old people. It is set on the exact spot where the Wallace family once lived—boys inside by the dozens, and Juanita's two girls sneaking in with pollen, coming home sticky between the legs, washing with the brown and white checked rag, stuffing it beneath the sink where Juanita finds it, a wad, and a story Juanita would not have if she knew it.

The old people are brought in from the outing to church in stainless steel carts and chairs. During their passage up concrete ramp, the steel of the carts and chairs glitters and catches in Juanita's windows. She feels each body ache, one dry bone rubbing on another.

Cynthia drinks her tea, chews the lemon wedges they have not used, her burning mouth an anodyne.

"Nobody loves me," says Juanita. "I feel nobody loves me."

"That's not so."

"I don't *feel* it," she says, thumping her chest, the head dipping down, light in the hair gleaming as if it were steel. Juanita's fingers dip into the Blue Willow tea cup, come out dripping sugar which she licks off. "If they did, I would *feel* it."

She wants to beat Cynthia's white, moleless chest, now or in the future. The scarlet blouse made of soft Dacron.

That night, Cynthia sleeps curled in the childhood bed, and what she dreams is not so much a dream as one of Juanita's stories which no one would have.

In real life, Juanita snores in the room across the tiny hall, the hair sprayed across the pillow, everything still more covered than the head.

Then, Juanita seems to rise, and she turns to Cynthia in a room which is old, paneled, high-ceilinged, and, for all that space, seemingly clean. A room in which no one eats.

Across the room is Cynthia's son as he was when he was nine. A young girl buttons his red sweater.

Turning, Juanita lifts her chin. Light falls on the bridge of her nose, and it is clear that this is Juanita five years from the time of this dream.

The teeth are high-yellow, that sexy color, and they grow apart from each other. The face pores breathe, each a gill. Red collar against a swan of a neck.

By existing, Juanita has surprised her daughter. And then Cynthia's breast bone splits, her breasts swing aside, and her body parts like a sea.

By the hand, Juanita leads Cynthia up the asylum stairs and into the room where Ann, Juanita's second daughter, spent three months. At the window, they wave to her. Ann is carrying her white laundry down the hill. The room, Cynthia sees, is so small not even five choir boys could gather at the foot of the bed.

Then, in sleep, Cynthia's body swings together again, catching Juanita inside.

Yet, sometime in the early morning, Juanita gets up and spits out phlegm into the commode. Paul, Cynthia's son, turns beside Cynthia in the childhood bed and begins, himself, to snore.

After breakfast, even though he is too big, Cynthia stands Paul next to her and ties the hood of his jacket. He is twelve now and comes to Cynthia's chin. She touches his face because it is smooth.

"Well," she says, "I guess that's it."

She sends Paul to the car with their bags, and he lets the screen door slam. Above that noise Juanita raises one hand to her widow's peak and says, "Really, that's how I feel." Waiting, she clears her throat. The bones in her chest move, the shadow of the crooked arm moves. "Still," Juanita says, "drive carefully and I'll see you next week, I guess."

"Well try to *do* something."

Then Cynthia and Paul are down the road and into the mountains where so many trees have been cleared for the road that the sun seems to exist only there.

Juanita's husband had come and gone at intervals, as if he had been visiting the poor, and so they remembered him as if he were always present.

Driving, Cynthia thinks, At his death I'll remove myself from him like a rib. She almost asks Paul, Do you remember him? The smile, his wide-brimmed hat, white, white teeth.

Their car eats miles; they run on hot dogs from roadside stands—hurry!—and Paul does not complain when Cynthia asks him to urinate in bushes by the road, even though he doesn't know why they hurry.

And when Cynthia remembers the man who must have, many times, slept with Juanita, she remembers him, even so, as beautiful. Except once, in a grocery store, she saw him break open—the grey suit, the white shirt, the maroon wool tie, Haines underneath, the wing tip shoes, the stuffed-in cigarillo, the mouth itself break open, and then no one would have trusted this man—crying and running up and down the aisles, a high, high voice belonging to a cat saying over and over "Oh" because she, his daughter, sat on the floor, holding her foot and watching blood pour from a wound made by a can of green beans falling from a shelf. It was as if suddenly he had gone queer.

Paul jiggles one foot crossed over his knee and watches for signs he knows by heart. Seeing this, Cynthia surprises him. "I want us to stop and visit your aunt," she says.

And Paul nods because what he knows has not yet traveled from his eyes to the brain cells, connecting. He does not remember, for instance, when Ann was thin, and, if he did, *how* thin, when the weight of the future could not be held in the palm like a plum.

"She's nice," says Cynthia, "and she's a fine cook," which makes two lies, a film coming into her mouth and spreading on her teeth.

They turn on Singleton Road where the apartments rise and block the sun. In a high window, Cynthia sees a woman standing between half-parted white curtains, and while the light is red, they wave to each other. "Who is she?" Paul asks. But Cynthia knows only that she is like them—her, Paul, Ann, Juanita, her father in the store crying like a cat.

"Well I swan," says Ann as she comes down the steps. Behind her hide the two children who are like each other but for their sex. They look out from behind Ann's skirt. "They're so silly," Ann says. "And will you look at Paul. Look at Paul," she tells her two, dragging them around before her, leaning over and cushioning them between her. "They want you to see their toys," she tells Paul.

Ann's boy and girl are like albinos, but Paul has never seen an albino and would not know if one were leading him up a stair. "We'll eat and then go," Cynthia calls to him. "We'll be home by dark."

"So how's it been?" Cynthia asks Ann.

"You know—this and that," says Ann. Ann wears silver and pink slippers with tiny bells on the toes, and she takes one-third of the couch. Leaning forward, she asks, "Did you see her?"

"She's all right. And you?"

"I would never be able to go," says Ann. "I wouldn't ever be able to go." And Cynthia discovers Ann's baby-eyes beneath the fat—the eyes she remembers seeing the day she and Juanita had found Ann walking through Asheville, North Carolina in a dress of feathers sewn to chiffon.

"I'll fix up something to eat," says Ann, wanting, possibly, to beat Cynthia's moleless chest beneath the scarlet blouse. A payment.

Cynthia watches her at the stove, sees her as the girl who was thin and barely covered, rocking herself in the hammock in Juanita's back yard, rocking, laughing and crying and holding her breasts because, at seventeen, a man had followed her home to touch her, even the doctor Juanita trusted unable to resist, seeing Ann when she was beautiful in feathers, rocking herself on the paper-covered table—touched her everywhere just as the Navy boy had done, and Ann laughing, telling her story over and over, rocking herself on the narrow bed where Juanita had put her while she was still laughing, Juanita saying, "It's got to stop."

"I wish you wouldn't stare," Ann says. "Eat." She goes to the door to call the children. Cynthia sees her half-hidden, sees, how much, framed in the doorway, she looks like a woman in an advertisement, covered and waiting.

Paul asks for the salt.

"I don't salt," says Ann, and Paul looks at Cynthia who shakes her head "No."

In the middle of the meal, Cynthia asks, "Do you have anyone, Ann?"

"No. And you?"

"Yes."

Then she and Paul are gone, up the hills and into the mountains which are small and into farm country where the roads make sudden turns, surprising.

"*Is* she nice?" Paul asks, and Cynthia says "Yes" in such a way that Paul will not ask again.

Cynthia imagines Juanita is beginning to prepare for bed, looking at herself in the fluorescent lighting of the bathroom, pulling down the bottom eye-lids, looking for redness or a white film, touching the moles which fester. "I'm so tired," Juanita seems to tell Paul, and Cynthia wants to cover his ears.

At a curve in the road, they come suddenly to a cow crossing—the warning sign beforehand, then the sound of neck bells tinkling against the spotted neck-fur. Paul with his window down, his head stuck out, a grin on his face for such a sight—cows by the dozens, heads following tails toward the milking barn. Across from the barn, which is set near the road, a large house sits in a cluster of trees, their branches jutting into the twilight sky.

"Oh yes," says Cynthia, cutting the car's engine and resting her head against the cool car window.

Then, far behind the cows comes an old woman in a house dress which reaches almost to her feet. Her gray hair is in braids and even in the muted light, it glows. Ann's fat; Juanita's age; the eyes of both of them, Cynthia sees; and Juanita's spotted skin. The old woman begins to sing to the cows, a rhythmical whine like crying and laughing—the voice cracks. "Look!" says Paul, as if the old woman were alien—the eyes and brain cells not connecting.

The old woman heads toward the barn. Cynthia starts the car and inches it past the fresh cow dung, the odor of cow, and the last sounds of their bells coming from the barn doorway. Then she sees the woman walking to the side of the barn, up the grassy ramp which leads to the hayloft and machinery. She slows to wave to the old woman, then sees a man who is young—young as Cynthia's father when she last saw him or Paul's father when she last saw him—step out to meet the old woman.

He pulls her up the last few feet of the ramp to him, and then he begins to touch her. He reaches down, almost stooping, and raises the long dress. He begins to rub the woman beneath the dress. He kisses her and touches the breasts which hang almost to her waist.

"Look!" Cynthia says. But Paul is rummaging in the back seat in the food hamper, and if he had turned around, she would have covered his eyes. *They were kissing*, Cynthia wants to tell Paul. He *touched* her, an old woman like your grandmother: what Juanita thinks of, thinking, Without some outside possibility, I would, right now, be done and over with it. Nothing notwithstanding, an incredible, yes!, flirting.

Then Cynthia and Paul are home though she had driven with only the picture of Juanita sprawled on a bed before her where the road should have been. Juanita carefully turns back the covers, carefully lays herself down on the bed, carefully lifts one leg. Her mottled chest is like Italian glass in the light which comes from the Home across the road. She is, seen like this—uncovered—ugly and to be loved. Juanita almost feels it.

Paul takes their bags in, then kisses Cynthia and closes his door. By the telephone, Cynthia looks at the room which would have had in it, and once had, a husband—how she sees him: waiting in a chair, the apron, which he never wore, still around his brown pants, and he is sleeping, breath going in and coming out as if he were a clock.

In such emptiness, Cynthia calls the man she knows, whose name also is Paul. And when he knocks, she had showered and comes still damp to the door.

He is not the kind of man who talks too much, and Cynthia could not imagine his wearing even an imaginary apron. He kisses her once, he asks, "Was the trip all right?" She nods and then he makes them both a drink. "I'm so tired, I'm so tired," Cynthia almost says.

But in her room, he puts the glasses down and touches her with cold fingers. Awake now, Cynthia closes their door. He has carefully turned back the covers, and carefully placed himself on the sheet, and carefully looked up at her.

Then, settling herself on him in the position he has taught her she likes best, she rides.

Lace

It begins with a wreck.

August bleaches the eye, a convergence of sun, humidity, the sight of dogs slinking under house pinnings as if they had been beaten, except their tongues dangle exposed and obscene.

The houses are narrow and white, like anemic ladies who, not wanting to presume, make normal women appear always sexual. And these houses sit close to the ground, their porches single gloves on burnt grass laps.

A lambent August. A minor wreck.

The cars are two Fords, one beige, the other grey, remaining dis-similarities subtle as skin texture. And it is true (an antecedent in the objective world which is retrograde): the beige car rams the tail of the grey car, as if this were the cause of what follows: the man in the grey car emerging silent, a long, almost fat razor in one hand; its blade catches light and flashes once.

From this distance, he looks like my uncles, the height of Rhett, that shaped back—my only view and proximity to him ever—and little Jessie's face, the side-view, so handsome in miniature it would make a nine year old girl wish she were a woman. He drags the driver of the second Ford out into the sun, which illumines his face: ordinary, *not worth remembering*, a confluence of everything forgettable about faces.

This face, this nothing face, and the car's color—beige like tripe—is why one man has predominance, is allowed to press the razor slightly into the

107

blue workshirt and steer him toward Lily's house. *Sympathy*. An old, old question, a profession of sorts.

> *No more tears, no more tears,*
> *We'll all be happy*
> *When there're no more tears.*

And, heading toward her kitchen, do men *know* Lily?

Facing the road, the kitchen is the first room, each subsequent room stacked behind the former like crackers, the bedroom last, and, in it, her iron bed, its feather mattress of blue ticking. Immaculate roses which will not perish clustered in a fluted vase on the mahogany table by the bed. Light enters all the rooms at once, a morning contagion of light.

They come in as if they knew her, the one whose face is forgettable leading, seeing first with the pale eyes her Sunday roast setting sliced and reassembled with string on the stove. The first hint of Lily, *Grandmother*.

Mother of these men?

They were, all three in the house, the same age. The age of compatibility, when the body is so taut it doesn't know the aches which will cause the serration, what amount of string bearing what possible tension will hold it reassembled.

Lily was brushing her long, brown hair in the bedroom when the man like my uncles and the man like nobody walked almost casually past the pantry and the sitting room and the wash room to stand arrested at her door.

Oh, I never saw her like this. A *bridle* of hair, the brush itself a restraining hand which she put down, turning.

Later, when she was 68, I saw the hand as a cloven hoof, death lambent on a day in January. The same roses; my father, *wearing his face*, standing down at the foot of the bed, arms folded across his chest as if they were suede, his face all nose, her dying a slow hunt. Lily was, riding that horse, three times the weight of *Lily*, until its jostling thinned her against her own bones.

Love: I would not believe her little story, or any story, or dream, which jumps time as if it were a stile, except: faces bloom, presenting, like clustered roses, fragrance, and the end of fragrance, the nose aquiver with faces.

The men and Lily looked at each other for what Lily said was a long time—a tableau of stillness, the three: interlopers in stopped time even as the sun moved and played its light on her hair.

Of the nondescript man, Lily said, "I never even really saw him."

But he is breathing, waiting to see what will be done to him by the inventor of this scene, who is growing taller now than he will seem again, power, no matter how puny, a rack with chains which stretch the frame.

"Jesus-Christ-God-Almighty," he says, to no one *in* the room, except his own taut body, "I hate, *hate*—if the son-of-a-bitch only knew—hate sniveling pantywaists who can't by-God drive a God-damn car, see?" Hissing, pointing with the razor. "So *you* get him, Lady—I wouldn't dirty my hands—and you *do* with him, and if you think I gave a good shit coming in here if you was a man or a woman, forget it. God!"

Lily. Who had never *had* anyone, who knew, mostly, how to cook, the ingredients of her own body unmeasured.

Then: he is gone. Taking his body with the miniature face, so handsome; and taking his little play worthy of the bottom-half of the Mason-Dixon divide where intelligence festers.

Lily *giggled*, one hand over her mouth as if she knew she would eventually lose all those teeth for the kind which sit in a glass. She lightly put the other hand on her belly, a reflex.

And it was then she noticed: *who was left in the room.* Later, when Lily was baying and my father was standing at the foot of the bed, she laughed. Death had treed that stranger like a fox.

A dream is not merely a dream; it begins with existing shapes, and my dream-children, although changed, later appeared in magazines, photographed, sometimes, across a double page. Now they are imprisoned in a chicken coop as large as Lily's house, the internal walls removed. All boys, all age twelve, stacked like loaves of Wonder bread on rafters, and, oddly, outside the day is ablaze equally with sun and the distant sound of guns.

Inside, how alive the boys are, each pinioned to his shelf with his own particular and engrossing pain, which does not scar the body outside; they are perfect boys. They are pictures of perfect boys.

They lie still and, but for what they feel, are as good as dead, which is, for someone outside the coop, for someone whose intelligence is itself a wound, the point.

And so, the boys, who are so beautiful, learn to make each raw nerve perpetually unthreading simply: his home. No one cries out. How proud their mothers would be! Would cry out themselves, *Oh Baby*, would want to wash the still features, undo this house. Missing the point.

For here comes the one boy who seems almost to fly like a hawk in the contrasting silence. Yet it is the slowest motion, each of the children feeling his own machinery absorb each feathered motion, the boy's face bright because, suddenly, he imagines he can find an empty tray, can trade that missing boy's pain for his own. Hurt less.

Which is impossible; someone has seen to that. And the children feel it, *futility*, and the one discovers it, an act of attrition for hope. Foolish! Every boy knows it: a blood tie.

And yet, they love him. Watching him fly back and settle, they love him, which I have dreamed over and over—the dream-sleep a perpetual beating of wings—regardless the boys appear different in the photographs, released.

Lily heard the screen door slam, the car start up and the driver backing it hard against the other car. Then the spin-off, an imagined flurry of dust distracting her.

She giggled again. She meant this stranger in the room to laugh with her. Then he would go, or, even, she could invite him to eat something in her kitchen, the two of them looking out the front window and talking about how dumb the other man had been, half-expecting him to return, to do something more spectacular, since he would by now be down the road far enough to begin thinking, feeling his neck chafe inside the Sunday collar.

"*Lord,*" Lily said to my father across the expanse of quilting where a thousand diamond-shapes lay muted in color. And he grinned, sheepish, because he never really knew what she was talking about. He was, simply, himself.

Dust seemed to settle in the little room, and then stop. Outside it was suddenly quiet—church-time, the dogs asleep.

"*Do* with me," the man said, his voice small, one hand-bell which he rang himself.

"*What?*" Lily looked at him again, tossing her head back as if the hair muffled his voice, moving slightly forward as if to pass him, watching him draw himself taller, moving as she moved.

His voice a baby's: "You have to. He *said.*"

"It was a joke!"

Later she asked for her teeth to be taken out, as if, telling this, she and my father, together on that hunt, had reached a stream where the scent might be lost.

"*Wasn't,*" he said.

Lily backed across her small room as he moved to the place where she had stood, her mouth drying, the tongue a dead clapper, and so she looked at him, his face a mote drifting on possibility, settling in one eye. Then, *graceful,* she slid under her iron bed.

"The last I saw of him was like that—he picked up the mattress as if it was nothing (her hands the curved toes of birds upside down on the wire), looking *down* at me like that. *Pshaw.*"

Lily put one finger in her toothless mouth where the tongue swam. She smiled at my father, the smile a buoy on her huge body.

"But, you know, Jimmy, he looked like you, and I didn't look at him anymore, but at the door he said, just as refined as you, '*Some*body will. *Some*day.'"

The South pinions a segment of its population, tradition without the money to back it up, culture residing in state capitols so remote it must be conjured in the mind's eye from the odor of cudweed on a hot day or the special yellow of salt licks sculptured by cows' tongues and the rain.

These were Lily's sons as they stood around her bed, waiting for her to be done with it:

Lamar: a milk truck driver for the morning run between Fair Shoals and Williamston, who looked like

Jessie: coal-tender on the Rockwell line between Anderson and Spartanburg, who looked like

Carlton: a pipe-fitter at the Lovell Space Heater Company in Pelzer, who looked like

Ronnie: a milk truck driver for the run between Fair Shoals and Williamston evenings, who looked like

Lewis: head engineer on the Rockwell line between Anderson and Spartanburg, hence, boss of Jessie and five years his senior, looking like

Rhett, whose face had, necessarily, to be remembered in these faces since he had gone to California to go into construction and had not been home since, and did not come to tell Lily goodbye.

And James, my father, the baby of them all, who was in that same little room the one farthest from her, her bed flanked by five versions of one face in varying sizes and ages (Rhett's an apparition almost flesh), handsome and not worth remembering, an eddy of faces from their father's side.

The crowd in the room thinned out as her body thinned; the months moved from September to January like a cortege, my father ending the procession, never moving closer, his eyes hound's eyes, which I came to watch, taking Lamar's place.

"And James," Lily said (in January, the bitter month), "*I always liked you best*. Now take my teeth out for good." And Little Jimmy walked around the bed and took them out, set them by the roses.

In waking-dreams, one's body drains away—as a hemophiliac's his blood—the objective world, not feathers the substitute but quills, and it could be Lily was, in January, featherless, borne away not on wings nor on a boat of bones but on these transparent spines, wondering

Who *did* with that boy?

And: *when?*

And never *if*.

Lily married a good man.

It took years before anyone suspected he was as good dead. An image like a tablet inscribed with laws, or like a tombstone, the body simply: down, also a graceful motion except it lacked interest, its opposite. . . .

Where is Lily's red taffeta slip, huge and thin as gauze?

If she opened her mouth wide enough, speaking in tongues, five warts wobbled there. The words mysterious, like panting, her sins locked in the confessional of her own language.

Sing for Lily "Abide With Me."

And for her husband "Just As I Am."

And James, who looked like none of the others, had one song, which would not stay the same. Sometimes:

"Lace, an apothecary jar,

five fish on an Ohio road

shining."

He was not a good man. He never did *anything*.

Or, he accomplished the ineffable; for instance, marrying twice and having the second time a boy whose picture I saw once when he was a baby so that the image of that boy—my only view and proximity to him ever—became the other half of the twin I had been, joined him not in an infant's death but in some other place, also a song, corny, and right out of that area of the country, in bad taste, except: it set me free. They had each other.

Lily never wondered *if*, even *if* it took her six sons with similar faces and all the Holy Roller Church could absorb in Greer, South Carolina before she got serious. Then: she took Little Jimmy with her, everywhere she went. Let him watch her grow huge and sensual and incoherent. A boy to stand at the foot of the bed. A mother needs such a son.

And *if* it ends with a wreck:

Sing for James' first wife, my own mother, this song: "She'll be coming around the mountain when she comes." Every verse a catalogue of what James *did*, beginning with *he left me* and, in the middle, what he said of her body: "If I don't get the goods, I'm not paying the money," and ending with *he left me*.

My mother arrives for a visit on an airplane of silver wings; if one is high enough, a hawk. *Hurt less.*

I send to meet her across the lobby James' grandson Paul. We see her coming in red: a coat of red, red lips, red hose, and, dangling inches below the coat, a dress the color of flamingo wings. And before I send him (he is built like a wrestler, age twelve), I imagine myself stooping to explain what I have acted on but have never said: *Your* father was a good man; but not *interesting*. Paul has under one arm *The Guiness Book of World Records*, his book of jokes.

So I push him on—built like a footfall player—and he has only heard her voice on the phone, which is not like her body: it ought to lie down; it refuses.

Then Paul sees her face, a filagree of wrinkles, no matter the red lips are painted into a smile.

I watch him stop, his shoulders drop, one hand in motion as if it might lift him up.

She squashes him, hugging: *Look at him, look at him.*

In the car, I reach back to pat his leg, to ease his first view of death. But Paul won't have the easing. Already he is a son to put at the foot of the bed.

And your mother is stripping down. She thins. And isn't it high time?

We take her in, unpack her bags—everything in them is a shade of red—and we feed her. Paul won't be kissed, a kiss would weigh him down.

His grandmother looks at his hands, saying, "You got your grandfather's hands."

"Whose?" Paul asks.

She laughs; James is *in* the room; Paul takes my place by the bed: she is that close to riding her body home, though she may go on for years, the years a cortege until Paul comes to stand at the foot of *my* bed. A face worth remembering: *he knows Lily and her son James.*

You see, Love: I know what I am doing: my own fingers loosening from the wire, one hand at my neck as I begin to undress when you visit, summers, jumping time as if it were a stile, and watch me unbutton the blouse, drop all the clothes, Paul listening through all the walls of the house no matter where he is.

Lord, you say, for the *life* of me.

And my laughing.

Litany (II)

for Billie Holiday

"Bodies, Love."

Phrase I cut from *Esquire*, pasted on the refrigerator door for Richard, of course for Richard, who severed one forearm on a moonless night in Greer, South Carolina in order to wake himself up. Wants me all his life to kiss the air through which the arm fell. He is so silly.

But the baby, God, the baby. Stolen. And I am so calm in that taking. *Dear Daddy, I am raising your only son because your last wife was too lazy to lift a finger.* What better theft than against the lie of laziness? You breathe: you own. Just keep breathing.

He is handsome as Daddy was, whose wives never marred him except to open up and drop lovely girls whose eyes ached; he noticed. Then, by the last of the wives: a boy. I call him Nathan.

"Nathan," I say to myself, "in a minute we'll go for a ride over to Greer to see my mother dying. You are going to watch her fall apart bit by bit and you're so young you won't know what hit you. Richard will come in with you slung over his hip, fastened by his one good arm, and the other, rounded two inches below the elbow, will become so familiar you'll be twelve before you remember, ask. And by then, Sugar, we'll be long gone out of here. Let's get started to Greer."

"Ready, Hon?" says Richard in the doorway, Nathan (did I not say?) slung on his hip. So we go, Nathan cooing over the uneven road.

My mother's face is wrinkles—a seal's face. "Lucy, Lucy?" she says in the

115

cool air of the garage house. *Where are Claire and Josie?* she wants to ask. *Gone,* gone sane, as they say. Got it clear that Daddy has died: Fact, an accident, no wasting, the body perfect but for one blue taint. So they took it at face value and went back to live like ordinary people. Their eyes hardly drift off. They go to parties, look for men to loosen them for just a minute. They meld, Momma. Now: see Nathan?

"Nathan, Momma," I tell her, pointing. "Isn't he cute?"

"Lucy, Lucy?"

So, as every day, we clean her up, spoon in the food. Nathan plays at her feet where the toes are numbing, and, after that, Richard lifts her up while I change the bed, and it's then I sling Nathan on *my* hip, his feet digging in *my* side. We take a long time doing this job and Richard doesn't know it matters who holds who while the sheets lift and fall. He's never asked why Nathan can't just play on the floor while I work or why he's the one holding Momma or why she can't be propped in a chair. How bright *is* Richard?

Then he drives us home in the pickup. I say, to keep him company, "Lawrence Welk's on tonight."

When we get there he goes out back to cut the grass while Nathan and I play in the front on quilts, for Nathan: natural vitamin D from the sun, sounds of the world, including Richard at his machine, and me.

My own voice is seeping out. When I can't sound high-tone, it'll be time to go. Class: you think no one thinks of class any more? When I talk to Nathan here in private, I am almost a lover, tight skin stringent for the near-perfect motion, that tease: the body and the world blend. What else are words for if not pretense the fish can't make? But for fear I'd like my own position, looking down into water at silver motion forewarning.

Naturally I scoop up Nathan and run to the back, calling for Richard. He always thinks it's the first time. "What?"—over the engine. I wave through noise and when it's finally quiet I step close in full light and I ask him, "Do I look older than my age?"

He squints.

"Thirty-two," I say, hopeful.

"No," he says, "I don't suppose. But it doesn't matter." Leans to kiss me.

He knows it matters. Maybe. I'm telling you: you should just see me *dressed.* Add that, on a city street—New York, Cleveland—to the eyes Daddy gave us and *that* is fashion. No stranger touches you.

"Nathan," I say, releasing him into the crib, "you are going to straddle the world."

And that night, just as Lawrence Welk comes on, I go over to Richard's

lounge chair, tilt it forward by climbing on, and touch my breasts, at which
he clicks the remote control and lifts me up. He has yet to see, since me,
anything on that show except two girls who stand beside the lamé curtain just
as Welk walks out—two months of only that curtain parting. *That* is power.
And all this time, Lawrence is aging. One day Richard'll say, "My God, look
at that."

Then, in bed, after the sliding on, I lift his short arm and ask, "Why did
you do it?"—a preparation.

"I don't *know*," he says, a moan. And then a look so dark comes in his eyes
it is profane and he makes love with all his mind. He could hold me. "Should,
should," I say, beating his chest with one fist—symmetry, sound. And when
it's over, I slide off and curl volitionally into the animal shape. When I'm
gone, he won't be the same. He'll be here and there. Some people don't know
what to do when they're finally ruined.

In the morning, I tell Richard what I always tell him after a night of love. I
say, "I wish Momma could just see this kitchen. After Daddy left her, she
would have loved it." Coppertone, Tupperware, the whirr of small motors.

I pack Richard his bologna sandwiches and send him off to work. At the
door he turns to me to say, "Bye, Hon," and then once more crosses the tile
to feel me up over my cotton housedress, to get me through the day, my
satisfied man. And, because I am perverse, I stand at the door and wave to
him in a certain style: the elbow bent, hand at shoulder height, the fingers
moving quickly in a wave just as I saw in a movie he took me to. And he could
care less. Lucy, I say to myself, your spit goes unnoticed.

Dear Sisters, I write to Claire and Josie who keep in touch with one another
discussing hair and skin and types of clothes, their assault on creeping age
which makes them, in some circles, perfect, and the men swarm, sensing
danger, *I expect Momma weighs 85 pounds this week, and the words are all
gone. She says my name, a sort of whisper. But no pain. Nathan is growing
and Richard is sweet as ever. I don't want you two to worry. I am fine.*

Then it is Fall, the leaves an Auschwitz of descent, color as indelicate as
blood in which Nathan and I walk as the afternoons close down early and the
sky separates into distinct parts. I sing to him, to all of him close in my arms,
and point out delights. Night-time we read together while Richard watches
T.V. in the den, and I say *together* because it is so: the squirming body on the
spread by me tuning up to rhythms from these books, getting his passage out

from my very mouth. Oh I am making him with a vengeance. Should I say aloud that me and Claire and Josie never liked sweet men?

How my mother falls (wet leaf, waterfall, striped awning, wings): Daddy said to her when she was twenty, "What do you mean, 'one place'? When we can have all of America?" Gliding her into the Packard, map like flowers laid across her flowering lap. And then, as if breaking off parts of states he'd never get to, he made us: Claire, Josie, me; tossed us in the back seat for safe-keeping.

And all that happened—I swear, all—was, once she gave him the certain wedding look as he closed the door on her side, walked around the hood which, passing by, he slapped once with the fat of his left hand, and slid in under the steering wheel, he found he needed that look more than once. Surprise, you know? which splits the body like an ax, which, in turn, invites itself in. He was a handyman. Sweet? My, no.

"Richard, I know why you did it."
"*Tell* me."
"Nope."

So I have here the dubious joy of hunkering: artifact and up-against-the-where-with-all. A dance, in mask.
For *what*, Richard.
For Momma *lingering*, Richard.
And if he is second-string in my weak phase—ballast for the tiny little bird's feet—well, he could catch me, too, if the arm business really worked.
Would never have worked.
But, Honey, if Momma is anything, she is testament to this: don't inquire too hard into your inspiration—a hand, leg, the wheels of Packard cars. So, sure, Richard, mercy, *have* us, me and Nathan-pure-as-toast. O Lotus, *hope*.

And then she dies. One full swipe, contiguous draining out. Claire and Josie: *Come*.
 All I want to know (strum)
 is how to eat (un huh)
 humble pie.

Delicately we laid her out. And, softly, I told Richard, "Once she was very beautiful. *Very*," that word a hissing, as if air from my mouth would lift her hands from her face—as we found them—and fold them peacefully over the chest. A folly. So I made my own arms soft, let Nathan's weight cover my chest as these two stems of daisies enfolded him. And Richard, pulling, released her claws; and I saw her eyes for that second, aching. He pressed them down, his fingers pennies.

And Nathan did not cry, nor Claire and Josie come to be with us. *Later* they came, for the ceremony. And Daddy's last wife at my request so that there, in waste, she could see Nathan one last time, show me a face of disinterest, which she did, gloved. And the ceremony was nothing—small and sweet-smelling, the sound of hems against pews, and whatever the minister said having nothing to do with Momma. So I brushed it off, as a skirt when one descends a bus, and, with the other hand, I waved my sisters out of sight—*two* hands needed to encompass such diffuseness. Claire and Josie will live a long time.

Three days later, I happened to remember Momma when she was a fury of loveliness: in a small clearing her Sheik had made in a wilderness *he* wanted to see, she nursed him back from sunstroke—the shivering toned by her flurry, and I was seven, knew enough to stand aside. And Momma ran—anything to pile on him. Her eyes themselves became ingenious, scientific, raked with knowledge. *Don't worry*, she whispered. As he thrashed, all the words he had ever learned came pouring from his mouth. And there, she had more of him than she had ever had. I promised myself I wouldn't listen, did you know that, Momma? (No, no.) And she saved him. Toward morning, she sat on the ground in the clearing and smiled. Then she fell forward into sleep. And it could be that *I* have not, since then, slept.

"Richard, she was *beautiful*."

Saying it to him, I curled, I became a female shape you do not see walking around. It began in the fingers. "Take Nathan," I said, "and see to him," and, handing him over to Richard, my arms curled, and my face.

After that, Richard did what he could. For weeks he cooked and cleaned and held Nathan. I don't once remember the sound of music in the house, or commercials. So: credit. And I tell you this in precise human calm.

But, Richard, THEN *you did not touch me.*

And now I want to say one does not take one's arm for oneself, no. Which, knowing the world, is what Daddy never knew.

And, why, Richard, did you THINK *I became a shape which frightened you?*

In sleep, my parts drifted off like separate schools of fish, as if I could cover, looking, every drowning space. I wanted Momma back and smiling. Which is impossible and which impossibility does not matter: listen to your bones. Nathan: *listen.*

I think it is what we have, the body, tuned.

So now it is done.

And, at the door (me and Nathan dressed, as I would previously have said, "fit to kill" because we want to keep our ears out there in the world—where else?), I tell Richard verbatim a woman's speech I learned on a late night movie. (No harm, Love, but in the asking and in time used. We breathe).

"For many things," I say, "I thank you. We will be fine."

And if he's *lucky,* as in *strikes* and *lady* and *good,* it will suffice.

Good

I am learning from my mother how to winnow.

Lois suffers, a sweat of suffering, and when she closes herself in the minister's office to cry (because it is his profession to deny the astonished Joseph, hope riding instead on a boutonniere), I wait on a pew with one hand cupped between my legs, the other curved over one small breast. So much noise I use it. And, behind me, the empty benches fill with mothers.

Winter: Lois is courted by a fat man who knew her when she was beautiful and, in a passion of remembering, sees the loveliness still. If he were to undress, the bones would be flat, the toes extraordinary little crimps, everything dry, reprocessed food. He has nothing between his legs, which I know because Joe rides me on the handlebars of his Schwinn out to a field, and what he owns rises against his belly—through all our clothes, I know the prosperous shape of boys. John Sr. doesn't like my eyes, which say to him, *Baby*.

He brings Lois perfect roses, thorns fruit-ripe, a danger on the mantle, signaling the coated glass. (Lois has a story she tells before that mirror. It was war-time, all the women at work, their play-things in trenches. Five in particular, with brushes they licked in distraction, painted silver on glass—there was a demand for hand-mirrors during the war. And, after some months, all these women, one by one in their separate houses where children slept in fatherless extremity, discovered in the dark, before mirrors, their bodies fluorescent with poison. And they died aburst with light.)

John Sr. sits under the mirror, by the space heater, drinking coffee, legs crossed at the ankles and the white, rayon socks showing. He says, "Good coffee, Lois," and, "It's high time someone spoke personally with the Secretary of the Interior."

Lois says of him (the amorphous), "He's good, you know," and puts on his ring, its stone a sixteenth note.

"He is," she adds (distracted), "the finest choir director in the state." South Carolina, where ambition knots the legs of service station attendants and magnolia blooms are initially fists.

And, *if* so, where is John Sr.'s grace, since we, who love music so, are, or once were, beautiful—non-toxic light—and Claire, who loves it most, is so graceful she hides from him, so fine at the piano she leaves me this fight, her tongue whole and resting.

Then he moves to the couch, indents it, and I have no place to sit. We will get sick and die. Between Lois's breasts dangles the emerald my father gave her, on leaving. When it swings out as Lois pours coffee, it catches music. Inside, her ribs are laced with stained glass.

My father is thin and wayward, the elements of a rainbow waiting to ease down, conditions now and then right. He keeps my heart bowl-shaped.

Wednesday nights Lois directs her own choir—the minister sings tenor; in her element, she tells him he is flat—and while she is gone, I help Joe feed his rabbits, which multiply as he presses my back into the wire mesh (after which time the hollow between the winged shoulders is a place few men can touch, as if it had burned). I run home as Lois's car rides over the railroad tracks, our forays into southern California a sunflower of noise on every axle. Slide into my window as she peeks in the bedroom door. She thinks the panting is her own body.

"Fool," says Claire, her swan's hair lost against the pillow-slip and the mouth webbing.

And this Claire, in February, begins an earnest dying, tired of hints—a fever so high it mats her hair. Everything stops. The shades, drawn tight against the windows, are angels. Joe doesn't touch me; he turns sweet and useless, and when I think of him as grown, I think he is a senator, pin stripes and impossible bills on the floor.

105 degrees—John Sr. takes himself away. *"Where is your father, where is your father?"* asks Lois, to which I shrug, because I have seen Claire smiling in her hot sleep, all our saviours shooed away by contagion; clean house.

When she awakens, she looks me in the eye and says, "I coulda died." Now, if you see her, fat and not quite ugly and dressed in royal blue single-knit pants suits, that will be Dayton, Ohio, in a warehouse, riding a

Huffy bike up and down the aisles as she carries invoices and sticks them on the tops of boxes with tape. But I am not sad, intent in her like a diamond.

Spring, and The Rainbow shifts from Alexandria, Virginia to our back yard, by the tomato plants, and he gets out of a powder blue Cadillac, and Claire, eyes all whites, gets up almost well.

"That man," says Lois, already wistful, breasts shifting, height her advantage as she loosens from the house and jumps the holly bushes, no matter that, later, he will push her into them and her wounded face will puff and redden.

He opens his arms wide. A gracious man. In my turn I hug him like who he is, and Claire, so lovely—fugues in her bones where marrow was—sticks out her right hand.

Days of Days—Lois sings and cooks and listens to the music of his belt buckle dropping on the floor, every night. I want Joe back. Inkling!

And what *if* the tomato plants die from my forgetfulness. My father counts the dried seedlings, my shame like apples. Oh, we eat *well;* we love him.

"Shit, no," he says to Lois, "I won't marry you again." (It is dinnertime around the oak table, our feet scarring its claws, one of Lois's 36 B pink bras hanging by a strap on the buffet knob, which means he chased her through the house and, merrily, caught her.)

You truly won't? Lois asks with her fork, it dwindling in the gravy, her right wrist a napkin.

Then, instantly, Claire is a bicyclist, taping her fever on—dying, we all know, makes words a balm. Fluff and apparition. Lois curses Claire in the fluorescent bathroom light and, innocent after dabbing that broad, white forehead (Gilead), says to Jim, "Move over."

We hear Lois's limbs untie, a respite by fire.

(No, I'm not sad. But *who* will lift Claire off the Huffy now, her two children at music lessons and her former husband asleep in his truck in Atlanta, Georgia?)

Jim washes his car and lets the food supply dwindle; cabbages, onions, potatoes consort in the dark bin, saying, *This is not it,* where is their pâté de foie gras?

In the trunk of his car are 8-by-10 glossy photos of women dainty as nurses. His suits hanging on a rod are, themselves, a business enterprise. In his glove compartment are tie stick pins, tiny rubies and diamonds like animal eyes closed in a hood of velvet.

Lois sews identical Easter dresses, by which she means to ease both her bells from the house at once—Claire's skirt is so thin at the waist it makes Lois say, *Look at that*. What does she know of bodies?

A Resurrection: his wholesome urge to move on. Lois cries, her eyes the stain of dogwood.

"I had a man, you know. While you were gone," Lois tells him. And he graciously (given) pushes her into the holly. His Cadillac, as it lifts over the railroad tracks, is a blue sky.

"*Where is your father, where is your father?*"

I shrug. And get sick—a quick study.

"Double-fool," says Claire, as no one nurses my head.

Lois installs a telephone. "Call someone," she says, but I don't want to talk when my body is in training, and Claire says she doesn't remember anyone.

Slowly Lois's face heals (formal silence) and I take a picture of her in her fleur-de-lis housedress under the chinaberry tree and, two weeks later, as if the developing company had tampered with time, the photograph shows her face on the downward fall, beauty slipping into the emerald. (What disintegrates first underground? My theory is the feet go last, in turn.)

Then it is May and Jim rides up in a maroon Thunderbird (the 8-by-10's are wives of second-hand car dealers). Lois doesn't move from her place on the couch—John Sr.'s hollow—and Claire is with Beethoven in the dining room.

I loosen and hug. "Well, Sugar," he says, "I do like that!" What he's good for.

"Out, out," he calls to Claire. "Both you go buy yourselves a banana split. I've got business."

At the Dairy Dream, I tell Claire, "One. 'A' banana split," to which she rolls her eyes and buys herself her own in order to leave it intact on the counter, pristine as I eat. (She is brilliant.)

Lois is a heap on the couch when we return; a gaggle of sobs moves down her body, her head turned in toward her stomach. My father is in the one good chair, smoking a cigarette. "Don't you ever let some air in this place?" he asks, and, in a minute, the room is filled with breezes and sunlight and the daisies across the road coming closer. "Well," he says standing, "you two sit." I sit.

He moves to the mantle, one arm on the ledge, his nose in profile. Claire watches this glass while I look at him, the real thing. He puts the Camel down on a saucer and clears his throat.

"It's like this," he says. "Seems the only decent thing, to tell you. Your mother (he indicates) has decided she has to kill herself if I don't stay, which, ah, I thought I better tell you. I'm not staying."

And the screen door opens, he's gone—a finger's click—the car's maroon dust ascending above the tracks as I go (softly) to close the screen.

"Really, Momma?" I ask, not knowing (*years*, not knowing) he has saved her, a broker liquidating certain stock, eye on the long-run. Claire says, "Shush. Fix her tea." Claire's cures: worthy of a long study in nuance—she dresses Lois in green, for lingering.

June, July, August—Claire stays in the house as I go off mornings for summer school—what I knew never appeared on tests ("She *seems* bright enough," says Miss Conklin to another as I stand on a ladder above them, tacks in my hand and in my mouth the letter "m" in off-red construction paper. "*Tell* me," she says when the other woman is gone. "I'd listen,"—my eyes her little rosaries as, almost, I flew down to tell her, except, looking— the last minute—I saw her buck teeth, which would have eaten down to the bone.)

Off, free. The bus puts me by the side of the road; I collect, I run, run! (my breath is seven colors) and go to a window, catch Lois *breathing*. Ha! I know what I know.

Could we use John Sr. now?

No. Not even now.

Joe: I have outgrown you. When you grow up, legislate for the millions and try, at least once a year, to appear on television, as they like that in our childhood district. And one more thing (unless it makes you bust a gut, in which case forget it), T.V. adds girth, and blue (in oxford cloth) is the only acceptable color under such lights. Listen to the women as their knees mate.

In September, the latter half, when the leaves are almost yellow and all the flowers disperse, Claire and I dress Lois fit to kill (black, and feathers around her face), take the emerald off ("Oh, no, do you think?" she asks, to which we nod, "Yes.") and the three of us (me in the back, their noses in profile as I straddle the middle) take Claire off to study with "The finest teachers in the state"—North Carolina, in the mountains, air good for T.B. but, winters, the fingers ache.

"She is so *young*," cries Lois, her back now in a brace and one hand on her head, always, and gas on her stomach from gulping air. "'Bye, Sugar', as your father would say. Do good and don't watch me cry."

I drive her home. (In time, we move; we move around—the South is a circle, and we don't poke out of it since we have seen the West and know to what virgin lands the rumors of decline and group sex apply.)

Claire, seen like that, is golden at a doorway. Four years she studies with the finest and, afterwards, she takes up with people who have afflictions you could point to: one in a wheelchair (Claire pushes), one with a missing hand, an accident of man or God we never found out, the question, don't you think?, inconsequential. A girl who shaved her eyebrows, which never grew back and she got tired of telling the silly story so that, by and by, people began to believe she was born that way. (Claire's husband, an inventor of the almost-possible—he was, like her, a genius—could have been traded in for two cripples: her advantage. But the children are very beautiful. People stop and, looking, remember beauty is fleeting. Fluff and burning. "Right nice kids you got there," said a farmer once. Casual. She prized that. What will her two think of her? I watch. I want to set them straight: *Your mother is, ah, a bicyclist for The Lord.*)

Oh, profane.

From my bed, I hear Lois's fat men come and go. They get just so far in the house (each house) and then one hand finds the line between her breasts. She says, "Really, I can't."

"You've Got the Personal Touch," sung by Lois —— (her maiden name) and dedicated to Jim —— (her married name). Her body dries slowly, her shame, a garden.

Now (yesterday and At This Hour) she is ugly, by contemporary standards. She ought not, again, to see Jim, who, on admiring the fountain in downtown Orlando, Florida had a local artist duplicate it in oils. From the fountain, amidst fine sprays of water, rises his portrait, the face Caucasian Guitar-brand. I preferred, that visit (*his* house), looking at him. I did like that. All mystery in one body, words not once applied to the meaning of existence. It keeps death close.

We call each other now and then—Lois, Claire, me. Thoughtful (breathing), they ask how I am. *"How are you?"*

I am well.

Done in my own oils.

My *feet* will be the first to go as, recently, I stood outside a college building in Georgia (small town where the get well cards gather dust) and listened, under pines and my feet bare, to an all-black choir (I did check) sing in the afternoon sun "Jesus On the Line." "Hello, Hello" and "Are You There?"

I was with a man I might not have worn out. (Habit tends to undo the outsides of things—oh, so: he and I were not ten miles, though we did not know it, from the hospital where Lois would let herself, again, be put under, let, again, something be taken out; so many extraneous organs! Hello? I ask Lois a month later. Are you all right? "Fine, fine.")

Traveling, I was with a man who thinks he is fat. Thinks he *needs* fat: heritage rich as drowning, four acres calling the birds, leather-bound editions, a phone which plugs in and out, boys who, if any, have a chance at staying beautiful, and their educations: a fine gauze. His voice so lovely (so full of wisdom it is best not to believe anything) and attentive to nuance it was itself a cure; how he took me half-kneeling by the kitchen stove (quiche lorraine), my back on the door and my shoulders: clipped, the hollow: unawares. Who can touch me now.

But (my dear, my dear), he is so very thin. And, if I could (what man would I not surprise?), I would tell him, for my own sake (as lying is a capital sin), how beautiful Lois is, when, on splitting her open (the daisies coming closer) one sees, inside, the perfectly-formed and perfectly-round, and tiny, bones of birds, along her spine a covey ready to fly out. She would, Lois ———, be ready to do it all over again. Lasting counts.

My feet draw up among feathers and disappear.

Clarence

Who do you love, Lucy?
Who makes my bones move.
How many men has that been?
Two. (And I want to know: what is grotesque, and will it come again.)

If (only) Lucy had remembered the place beneficially: cow bells, the odor of dung, cudweed, hay, the high-C of metal pails hitting on one another as, behind her, inside the house, her aunt sang *Oh my lover is a fisherman and he lives on the big, blue ocean. / In his little boat, in the crimson sun, he goes out with the tide each morning* (crimson of silk scarves, Rasputin under candles, of tight nylon blouses, or reefs), Romona's voice high, the song a cappella and beautiful although the singer herself was fat (and thereby ugly). And Clarence (uncle: bird of judgement): thin, so, in his own right, ugly.

Lucy, chronologically almost twelve, the body sidling up to rampancy, sat on the stone steps. Twilight disappearing under the mountains (the fisherman under the roof of his fish), which drew the roads in after them, the air a quilt. You could sleep, if you had a place; but Lucy beds down in her uncle's house inside two Queen Anne chairs, against brocade, and when they slip apart as she turns in sleep, she dreams she is being sawed in half—in the morning they find her parted in the formal setting, between four lace doilies. And the dream, as with the makeshift bed, seems temporary.

As if she were tired, although she is never tired, she sighs. What is her memory unthreading along the arms and down the spine to the toes—

translucent silk threads, which align themselves along the nerves; so memory is not wholly stored sights and sounds and what the hands have touched, but: breathing. *Lucia.*

Romona comes to the door, the song still among the ribs and sliding into her name for Lucy, "Lou-cheeee-ah," and she throws open the screen.

"I'm here," said Lucy, her voice precise (precision enough the pick the bones clean—Romona, why aren't you starving yet?).

Romona, looking down, stopped by the voice and by Lucy's silhouette, arms wrapped about her knees, hair unbraided, falling to the stone steps ("They'll never know what it cost me to have all of them here; won't ever *guess*," is Romona's refrain later).

"One day I might read you some William Blake," Romona said, which lines were wasted on Clarence, thinness a taut canvas. "Would you like that?"

"I guess so," said Lucy. "Who's he?" (Which now she knows, 22 years later. Unfair, to be caught by remembered benefice—honed edge on the strop of nerves. Some words, Lucy says, crack the body as if it were ice—*bien*, when the pronounciation is clear and soft.)

Romona had let time pass, looking down to the barn (Lucy's left arm bunched between her knees and chest as she moved her hair around one ear), and then asked, "Are they coming up soon?"

"'They'?"

"Your father's down there, with the dog. Clarence won't like it."

Lucy has not heard her father drive up; and when? And why did he not first come up the hill to the house, come in business-like and handsome—whitest teeth, straightest nose, a tan so subtle it would not remind anyone of work or of Florida—such style anyone could see that Jim (the clean name) could, when he wanted, get his family out, down the road to some other place. Then the road itself is a place.

"Well," said Romona, "I'll go in."

Where is my mother. She is curled on the day bed, atop the covering of green and red plaid canvas. Morning, afternoon, evening. She says that she is resting. She says that she never sleeps. I sleep (morning, afternoon), and what is real settles behind the eye, dream-mote, and at night we come out, splitting carnival act, the crimson blouse, lights: beams of lights. My mother is dying for the stardom sleep.

Lucy waits for the barn to brighten—one narrow window opening on to each cow's stall as, tentacled, machines draw out the milk. There is no moon, the dog quiet (Sheba, the *Queen* of Sheba), Romona in the recess of the kitchen, odor of squash and onion.

Then, lighted, the cows' heads are portraits, and it is too far to see also that they are chewing. Lucy scratches one leg. It is almost peaceful. "I love the quiet here," Lucy's mother, Pauline, said one morning. "Your aunt is a lucky woman." Romona leaves her cooking to put on the player a recording of *Carmen*—"Listen, Lucy"—Carmen as Romona, and she dies in English, blood an anodyne for passion. "Listen."

Maybe Pauline is rising (because Jim is down at the barn and Pauline knows it by how the air itself changes) and comes to stand at the doorway, watching Romona at the sink, the fuchsia rayon housecoat (ribbed in navy blue, which makes it almost tasteful) not tied but wrapped across her belly with her arms. She is thin (and pretty). "Are you going to eat something tonight?" Romona may ask her sister. The tomatoes cape-red, seeds afloat in juice, so much frying in the air: excess and weight, the ponderousness of one place.

It was then, as Lucy was caught in reverie—*Pauline is a tightrope-walker's net, the holes are indolence Jim falls through, and lives*—that she saw Jim's car shooting rear-first up the delivery ramp from the barn, the headlights as he backed out and turned flashing over her once. He stopped, throwing open a back door to let in the dog. ("But Pauline," Romona had asked once, "aren't the children unstable?" "No, no," Pauline had said, "they have the dog." She had paused, blowing smoke from her nose, leaning slightly forward, as if puzzled. "You see.")

Then he was gone, tires raising a dust which almost settled before the one sound from the barn, of a metal pail being thrown, hard, against a concrete wall. The cows bellowed; Lucy could see the headlights of the car as he went over the bridge. Finally, nothing.

"Well," she said aloud, "I'll go in." *Waiting.*

In the kitchen, Lucy slouches in the doorway by Pauline and listens to them: "Sliced tomatoes, you think?" "Oh, I don't care, whatever." Dropping her arms across her belly, like Pauline but without the robe, and it would be years before she remembered just when she had begun to adopt the mannerisms of Pauline. "Well, we will, since the garden overgrew and we're swamped." "I suppose," says Pauline. The robe precisely parted.

When Lucy is 33, she pictures for the first time Clarence as he must have appeared when he threw the pail. She is standing by a car, keys jingling (twilight a fur behind trees) so that the sound ran from her fingertips and down and up, a shiver, though she is now: a lady. His thin arms where veins bunched like muscles on the pink, inside skin without hair; and his face muscles tight along the cheek-bones, the false teeth perfectly aligned as they clamped, the little chest puffed, and the loose, forest green pants bagging at the knees as they bent with the throw. No hair but a black fray at the collar, his face red and the eyes swallowed in black. *Clarence was five feet, five and one half inches, so when he finally shrank into the wheelchair, who noticed but me?* This amber thread (color of all the sky), until Lucy rested her head on the warm car hood and, suddenly, wanted to be held (a sliding holding) by either man she loved.

Either?

Oh yes.

And if this set of bodies, so conceived, is shameful, Lucy does not know it.

Clarence came in when the chicken was done (dry bone loose from skin, the smell changed), wiping his feet on the back stoop mat and his hands—they are clean—on his green pants, his head dripping water from the porch faucet. He looked at Pauline. Possibly, from where he stood, light played on the folds of her robe, a line down to her bare feet. She was smoking and, Lucy saw, was engulfed and padded. He walked past Pauline as Romona called out, "Soon, so don't go cutting off my music."

Lucy slips off her ballerina shoes and, looking down, splays her toes. *No one here pays attention.*

The tablecloth is white linen and, behind Clarence and Romona, a set of white curtains flutter. The plates are brown and before each plate sits a tiny swan whose ribs hold salt. The glasses are crystal with fleur de lis chiseled around the bowls. They all—a sideboard of women—sit with their hands folded in their laps, no napkins but these hands. Clarence lifts one hand and places it by the plate of okra. The chairs are ladder-backed, so on either side of his shoulders, Clarence grows white-painted spindles. Romona sweats a residue of kitchen heat and with one hand balloons her sleeves. ("You can't smoke at the table, is what I don't like," Pauline said once, in private. "Which is from my mother's side.") "Well," said Romona, "we going to eat, or what?" Clarence clears his throat.

He said: "Now pay attention. Because I won't have *any* of you thinking that because Jim doesn't always eat with us that's why he's not eating with us tonight. No. He's not eating with us tonight because I was down at the barn and I walk into the cooler room and he is reaching into the cooler and he takes out a quart of Guernsey milk—I stand and I watch: he pours the cream off the top, a good five inches, and he gives it to the dog and then he reaches in the cooler and he takes out a quart of Jersey milk and he gives the cream off *it* to the dog. Puts the lids back on, puts them back in the cooler, closes the lid, and pats the dog. I told Jim, 'You get off my property and don't *ever* let me see your face again as long as we both shall live. I work,' I told him. 'I put you and one of your kids up and *her*, because they're sisters. I *work*,' I told him. So that's the story. You'd think no one had ever spoken to him, that's the kind of man he is.''

They eat in silence; the record needle runs against the spindle and, even as Pauline clears the table before her after-dinner cigarette, no one lifts it off. It is like a cricket in the house. *Lucy. Lucia. Thinker and darkness.*

And, the whole time, Jim had his clothes in the car and, lined up on the driver's side of the dashboard, a toothbrush, can of tooth powder, little hand-mirror, castile soap in a brown penny-candy bag, and his razor. A book of three-cent stamps. Pauline could be out on the daybed, burning tiny cigarette holes in each place red weaves over the green, knowing Jim's letter's coming. When he's ready.

The day Pauline washes her robe she rests in her pink acetate slip with the beige lace and draws the filagree curtains leading from the porch. When she gets up to sit in the rocker, she looks so thin she is a wing of silk.

One day when it is so hot even the cows stand apart, Lucy visits her as the robe flaps drying on the clothes-line. On the floor, painted the color of redwood, are all of Pauline's things from the pocket of the robe: Coty lipstick, pearl nail polish, a hairbrush made from boar bristles, and a pair of transparent nylon panties. Pauline sits with a letter open in her lap and she looks past the barn where the sun hazes the sky. "Sukie wrote. Want to hear?"

Cynthia, Cynthia.

Lucy stands behind Pauline and plays with her hair. "Read it in *her* voice."

"'Her voice?' What do you mean, 'her voice.' I'll *read* it. You go over there and sit. Now: this is dated a week ago. But the postmark is three days ago. So, either she forgot to mail it—carried it around in her pocket—or she thought about it. Which do you think?"

Cynthia is too thin and pretty to think; she isn't even there. Lucy paints one fingernail. "Am I going to be pretty?"

Pauline rubs her eyes with her hands and turns to look at Lucy. She looks for a long time as Lucy stills her body. "I think," says Pauline, "I think—but don't ever repeat this—you'll be worse than pretty or beautiful. I think you think too much. How's that?" Pauline laughs: *lights, beams of lights.* "Now here it is: 'Dear Momsie (ha, ha), I bet anything you're mad. Grandma gives me every day a whole quarter to spend. I get a R.C., a Sugar Daddy, and Necco wafers. My teeth will all rot out. We went to Holy Rollers and I got saved, but don't tell Lucy. I get to sleep on a pallet on the floor. Yesterday I pulled weeds and we took the cart over to Greer and I made $1.35 on my tomatoes and squash. I bought *True Romance* and read it all. And some see-through panties. You better come get me soon. Love, Cindy.'"

Pauline folds the letter and smells it. "So how's that for a letter? Now go *play*, Lucy. Go anywhere you want. I am so tired."

When Romona practices at the piano ("I Got Music" and "My Man" and, sometimes, "Strangers in the Night") Lucy stands at the window in Romona's bedroom, looking out to a rock patio and, beyond, to the cedar tree split long ago by lightning. ("God, the fire!" said Romona. "It was so strange—rain and all, and the top of the tree burning. Then it stopped, and it's been that way ever since.") Looking out at the tree and feeling behind her the presence of Romona's clothes, trunks, sachets, Lucy feels sandwiched in. What do *you* know of love, she repeats, a phrase from Pauline—gift, fruit. *Where is Jim. Now, I mean.*

She began to go through Romona's drawers, the closet, the trunks—not trying *on* the clothes (so many shades of pink, textures of light) but learning them by touch—such weight in their expanse, as if all the house were in one dress, Clarence up one lace cuff. *He* had almost nothing. At the window, she tries to feel what he owns, and then she looks: nothing. Forest green pants, one suit coat, white Haines sets folded in sets, forest green shirts, and six white handkerchiefs with a green aligator embroidered on one corner. *Where are the pants to the suit coat?* One wine-red tie.

Romona's powder is a constant dust in the room which the sun lifts, as if Romona had settled on the bed, her short feet propped on the satin pillows, her head propped on satin pillows, her body a boat-shape. *Clarence sleeps on the side by the wall, Clarence sleeps on a pallet on the floor, Clarence comes out of the closet under moonlight when it beams through the burned cedar.* Lucy dusts herself with Prince Charles and, before the mirror, unbraids her hair.

Today, precisely what does a pint of heavy cream cost?

Guernsey or Jersey? No. I mean: Two is so very few.

Lucy found a boy at the farm past the bridge. A year younger. Ray. ("Remember Ray?" Romona asked years later at a reunion. "Well, he got married young. Couldn't wait, that's what they said: 'Ray just couldn't wait.' You know anything about that, Lucy?" Romona never smoked, not one cigarette in a long life.) And, with Ray, Lucy practiced kissing. Back against tree bark, small knobs like warts through the cotton dress, her eyes shut, teeth-on-teeth, always in a place where it was sunny so, through her eyelids, she saw, if not him, some shape, until, finally, she found his tongue and taught him. (Years later, to contain the body, one of Lucy's two men, not knowing what to do with her, precisely what he was to do with her since he had, unaware, given Lucy's place to another woman and now, meeting Lucy, understood what is worse than pretty or beautiful, and did nothing, restraint itself a place beside him, once lifted Lucy's dress and kissed her, once, on the belly. Then let her dress float from his hands, settle in its own time where his mouth had been. *Of course I know what happened to Ray.)*

"*Talk* to me," said Pauline to Lucy. It was almost September. Clarence had begun to act as if they were not present, and so Pauline had begun to take her meals on the porch—oatmeal, with heavy cream, served in bowls with handles and, other meals: Romona's plates of color. And, after one meal, Lucy joined her; otherwise, without Pauline—kinship close as clothing—Lucy watched Clarence's chest hair sprouting around his green, open collar; or Romona's fat hands, the one ring set in the flesh so deeply it was almost lost. "I wish you all wouldn't do this," said Romona as Lucy carried her bowl from the dining room. "I wish . . . ."

"Brush my hair for me, Lucy," Pauline said.

Then Jim wrote.

Pauline takes the letter in at lunchtime and, standing by the table, tells Clarence, her voice dry and her hands, Lucy sees, shaking. "He says pack up the trailer, then in two weeks we'll be going to Buffalo, New York, wherever that is."

"Jim works," Romona said to Clarence. "See there?"

But Clarence has two hired men fill the trailer. "Tell Jim," he says to Pauline, "to meet you down at Jordan's gas station. We'll get you that far. He can pick you up there."

Lucy walks through the house, ending in Romona's room. She rests on the bed and, after she is rested, stands at the window and feels behind her, for the first time, everything Clarence owns. The forest green of lingering.

At Jordan's Pauline smokes and drinks Cokes. At ten-minute intervals, she goes to the ladies' room to check her lipstick and dress. "You look like a movie star," says Lucy. And, just before it is time, Pauline puts on a black felt hat, curving the brim over one eye. *Bien.*

The trailer sits by a pile of used tires, where Clarence's two men unhitched it. Ray comes by to watch, toeing the dirt. "Well talk, Stupid," says Lucy, but, of course, Ray has nothing he can say. Lucy gives him a ribbon from her pigtails.

"Sweet," says Pauline. "Isn't Jim ever coming? I wish Romona was here."

The sky is the color of tumblers' mats, trees in the distance are turning, and, at four, early because of the sky, the owner of Jordan's cuts on the lights. Sometimes Lucy can see the owner look out the station window at them. They are hungry with waiting.

Jim drives up waving. Pauline was reading a chart about tire mileage, her back turned from the road, so Jim honked his horn twice. Running, running—Pauline throws down her purse and runs; he gets out and lifts her up, twirling her around; Pauline is crying. *Do not cry, never cry,* says Lucy to herself from where she waits by the air pump. And when Jim sees her, she notices he will last forever.

"Well, Sugar," Jim says. And Lucy lets herself be scooped up. Sheba barks in the back seat of his Packard.

In Landrum, they stop to get Cynthia, and she comes out of the little house as thin as she went in. *Not saved, not ever saved,* and, although her weight went up and down with the years, itself a circus act at ground level, anyone could see it was not a saving weight. *Sometimes, Cynthia, I call you Sukie to myself. If your hair were its rightful color, it would be gold.*

"High time," Cynthia said, and she climbed in the back seat.

And then, ostensibly, they were gone, the road the place they knew best, and, for a long time, because Jim told them to, they believed in adventure. Jim rested his hand on Pauline's thigh as he drove.

Why those particular men, Lucy?

I don't need to know.

But, later, Lucy tries to remember the house in Buffalo, New York, the length, even, of the street itself. She dreamed a house, but, always, inside it was the set of brocade chairs, and, always, she slipped apart in sleep.

And when Lucy asks Cynthia (and never asks Pauline because, tiring of adventure, costumes of madness, Pauline went to live alone in a place Jim only stopped by on the way to some other place) to remember with her the house, Cynthia swears in *that* house she slept on a pallet on the floor.

Everyone who ever knew Jim saw him now and then.

But never Clarence.

In time, Clarence grew fat. He began to choke on food. At any time, day or night-time, Romona (growing thin and beautifully old) might be on the mountain road, driving him blue-faced to a hospital. Under lights, the doctors reached in with their fingers, with tongs, with suction cups, and drew out the food. In time he sank into a wheelchair and, in time, the doctors named a disease.

One day he would be eating—slowly, carefully—the softest food—and he would turn altogether blue, face falling into the bowl with handles, breath coming out his eyes like steam. *I can see it now*, Romona wrote to Pauline. And Pauline let Lucy know this picture: *kin close as tights, interrogations under lights, the noble heads of spinners-by-teeth as they fall.*

Jim drives from state to state.

We love him, isn't that right, Pauline? Lucy hears her say, "Oh, I suppose."

Clarence (fat and in his own right ugly): *villainy is an act of omission, after which some bodies float and others, filled with holes, are useless.*

What, Lucy (softly), do you need?
I need not to have to talk.

Louie and Althea

for Donald Barthelme

(Bodies of different weights fall with the same speed in a vacuum.)

It was hot. A bad night if one had trouble breathing, and Louie, with his pea-sized lungs strung close to a heart the size of twin persimmons (enclosed in a cage like a cricket's), moaned into his pillow and asked himself what Althea, the freak, was doing on such a night.

But, really, hot or not, he liked thinking of her and wondering why she was a freak, which surely she was, and when he could expect an answer to this question which plagued him. Cursing, cursing this intellectual's bent, as if the mind bloomed in a hollow where the gnomes lived, not in his body—swamp of a thing and dangerous. Out there, it was airy, a place he might, one day, take Althea for a walk, spin her in a grove and kiss her dried-apple lips.

Althea talked all the time, applied ointment to the cracks in her lips, and kept on talking without knowing why, but, otherwise, was lovely. And, being lovely—with all that vanity which is like a cavern or a warm bath or finding six fish placed side by side in the middle of a road when a haze is over the sky—she never really looked at Louie.

As it was, she felt she never really saw anything the way she might if she could get her mouth to stop working, since, with that blur going on at the end of her face, she felt distracted, as when gnats play around your eyes.

She turned on her bed and sighed, and let the trickle of sweat run unattended into the ointment.

It was an October night, with its last surge of an Indian-summer heat, when any person who has minded the time of his body feels frost climbing up the legs, and knows that when it reaches his heart he will feel sorrow if he has not properly loved and been loved in return.

The man who owned the big house knew this truth and sat, on this night, in his red wall-papered library and wrote his mother a letter.

"Dear Althea,
   You always talked too much, but this is to let you know I loved you even if I could not get a word in."

Maybe Louie sensed Althea would crumble when reading the letter from the man in the big house—since everyone knew everything about Althea (as she told it all) and knew, except this son, how much she had wanted to let him get a word in. Which is what such October nights can do to a person who might, on any other night, remember words are not so precious to be serviceably employed, not like diamonds on a witch or a yellow hat on an albino.

Louie rose and paced across his trailer. He opened one of Althea's perfume bottles and sipped his own home brew. His little heart raced, his feet started up, and he ran out of his trailer into the October night. He could hear both Althea and the scratching of a fountain pen, way across town and in the dead center of the house, through all the red wall paper. He could hear crickets and a man in Tulsa—miles away—snapping on his drawers. Ah well, he thought, what is there to do? And he took a walk.

"P.S. Althea," the man wrote, "it isn't that I blame you, and, really, I should have loved more persons than you. But, really, isn't that beside the point, I mean, things are as they are, wouldn't you agree?"

Louie walked past the bakery where he could hear the sourdough rise, and past the brewery where other yeast worked, and into an open field where the moon breathed down a stump. He stood on the stump and danced, but it was no use.

Althea turned in her bed, loud with self-recriminations, and then she, too, following her own breath—onomatopoetic with the hiss of flies and the scratching of crickets—went for a walk.

"It's not that there was anything in particular to *say*," the man in the red room added. "It's simply, well, there should have been a *pause* after you said—I've forgotten—all those love-noises mothers make. And, in that pause, I could have said, 'I love you too, Mom,' and that would have been a great, an enormous, *relief.*"

Louie, hearing all, thought of how few people he himself had loved, because, mostly, in the lapses, they breathed wrong or laughed wrong or let on in some way they didn't know at all what they had been talking about. And this fact, maybe known only to Louie made Louie sad on such a hot and miserable night. Only Althea seemed to him pure. Because Oh! if she were to stop talking, for just one tiny minute, it would be as if the heavens had opened and the silence of the angels ensued.

As it happened, Althea came upon Louie out in the glen where the moon and the heat were at cross-purposes. And, on seeing Louie, whom she had never really before looked at, she gasped and held her breath for one longest minute.

It was lovely!

And then, Althea began to beat Little Louie to within an inch of his life, saying all the while that he looked, in miniature, just like her son whom she had never liked at all.

Which is by way of saying, Louie was mostly right—like any man, and Althea talked too much—as all women do, and that, as we may have suspected, the man in the big house tore up the letter to his mom and fixed himself a toddy before retiring.

Children

It is noon when Claire begins screaming, the high-C of arch suffering (history and waste) in a repertory which will never contain cancer of the bone marrow or one lost eye. So: who cares? Except, afterwards, her body will not look quite the same—puffiness under the eyes and on the belly a mound of fat and in the shoulders what looks like fat but is instead a realignment of wings—clipped, a curving inward like a second set of ribs protecting a second stomach, and she slows down, as if chewing thoughtfully. If anyone were watching, he would pause, the repose of any animal sensing a foreign species, its habits embedded in the brain like teeth.

And her piano playing goes—trash like tin cans on a marriage car, and Helen, her mother, is seen afterwards opening her hands as if to let loose a basketball, saying, "Well," meaning *one never knows* or *imagine that*, just short of it taking all kinds: Claire in her new life not air around any instrument but a secretary, backdrop a pastiche of all white, Claire in bas-relief of bright aqua and the purple of grape juice. What Claire says to the girls at lunch is, "Let them see me coming and going" and "Oh God, my hair, what a mess," which now is true.

And Claire's two children trailing behind her like wooden boats on a string and the missing husband driving his pickup around and around a surburban Atlanta A & W root beer establishment. Helen doesn't catch the images of water, says, instead, "Life, you know?" afterwhich she closes her hands and studies the ring finger.

Impedimenta spelling *defeat*, except no one will have it. Claire's pupils jump, volley of attention atop a slow weight. Can the eyes purify?

Now, almost noon. So Claire calls her sister Lucy on the house phone across the scratched marble floor and says to her in the softest voice, "You are the shit of the earth." And while Lucy holds the phone before her as if it were a third hand, a fourth counting the bones in her spine, Claire begins screaming behind the switchboard operator's partition while the guests stop and lift their heads, ears cocked like dogs'.

Then Claire, in black, runs out, trailing behind her the tentacles of the headset, which make a sound like six little feet on the marble floor. Lucy, for a long time, thinks what she sees behind the double glass doors of the hotel is Claire's dress from which the appendages have been separated when in reality it is a concrete block wall painted black. Turning, she sticks her hands into the cooler among the bottles of quinine water and their shaking makes waves across the bottle caps.

At half-past, the manager has Lucy sitting on a Naugahyde sofa across from his desk behind which he sits tilted forward, listing, saying, "I don't quite know how to say this. I think your sister needs—let's see—*help*."

But you, my dear, are a fine and outstanding worker, quiet, with your head in the right place and, if there were birds, they would lift your curls at the nape of your neck and kiss you there, *so, of course, you can stay on, we aren't heartless here*, know a good family name when we hear one even if fortunes have turned; jewels still spill from the hem of your dress; how strange it must be to have them fall around you every time it is lifted! Ah Lucy, Quiet Worker.

"'Left?' What do you mean, 'left'?" says Helen at the curb when she picks up Lucy at six. So she double-parks; her red heels move across the sidewalk like tandem ants, and in five minutes she is down from the mezanine office saying, "'Left'? What does he mean, 'Left.'" All the black people at the bus stop turn and look and Lucy, because she can't stand Life when Helen goes into action, waves to them as Helen shifts into second, saying, "Well, we have to *look* for her. You do realize that, I hope."

And what Lucy realizes is that not even Helen can conceive of the screaming, higher than lutes. They are, then, looking for someone quiet, pasted in a doorway.

Night-time, Helen is pitched across the brocade sofa, crying. Every once in a while hopefulness makes her lift her head and say Claire will *pay* for all that gas. *Every ounce,* which becomes a litany. Light rests in her hair, thin and fluffed on the bolster. The part is red. Relatives, alerted, are calling and, at intervals, Helen gets up to say, "No!" her voice one key. "And the police won't do a thing. You know what they say? They say she's 'of *age*.'"

What do *they* know, is what her look says when she cradles the phone and rests her head again.

Concession: it is true. Claire, right now, is beautiful and thin and capable of a "Moonlight Sonata" which makes even Helen stop talking—Claire carries its sound in her eyes, the blue, startling, cushioned by the tiny vein lodged at the root of her nose. Skin and hair: ivory. They don't know *anything*.

The Doctor Claire will see later—essential but seemingly an afterthought, as may be the way of anything essential—is across town, sleeping under sheets which smell of bluing. Anderson, South Carolina, where the good are dead to the world sooner than most. In this case, his sleep is a reprieve.

Lucy stirs at the doorway where the porch light is on so that Claire, out there, can see her from behind the willow where Lucy imagines her resting, Lucy's hair (always a mess) framed in the top section of the screening. Bugs circle the light and, behind Lucy, Helen raises herself on one elbow and in the lucidity of early morning hours says life is a vale of tears.

Two days later, Lucy will call Tampa, Florida and her father will say, "'Lost'? Well *find* her."

How he got where he is.

And he will add, "I told your mother, more than once, as I recall, I said: Get that child out in the *sun*." Lucy will remind him (from the closet, hidden with the phone among Helen's dresses which she fingers in the dark) Claire's not like us. And James will say, "The hell she isn't. I don't understand this 'grey area' at all." Then hang up, the local news on his mind—hurricanes, and will the sand bags hold.

Someone knows something.

Even if it isn't James, who, on putting down the phone makes himself a note to send Lucy for her graduation a Longine-Wittnauer watch, which he does, and, much later, when Lucy is living alone with only her boy for company, who is so fine a child he makes her chest ache, their cat will be playing with the watch and Lucy will allow it, her arm feeling for the first time airborne. And that day she will send the Doctor a picture of her son dressed in a playsuit she has made herself, time plump.

Pacing through the house, her motion making the four rooms jump as if in transit, Helen stops mentioning the wasted gas. After work, Lucy reads to Helen from the Bible, all the cheering passages although Helen reminds her they are *extractions* and by no means *the whole story*. Helen rolls her eyes heavenward. Lucy asks, "Where did you go looking?" and Helen says, "Out by Whitehorse Road."

And with six days gone by (Helen telling the area manager of the jewelry company she sells for that she can't possibly come in "until something happens"), they can both picture Helen in the car more easily than they can remember Claire: for instance, who's *feeding* her? On the little finger of her right hand is the initial ring she got when she was five, her fingers so graceful they are themselves a pirouette.

Helen's voice goes strange. Relatives who drop in with casseroles as for a wake say to each other she's falling apart.

And Lucy thinks she herself should have studied piano, fear for Claire about to become an art work. "We can't take much more of this," says Helen. "I trust Claire knows that."

Then Lucy, as if to tease herself, lets Claire slip through her hands—or was it apparition, Claire in lilac. (Even the Doctor, in a fever which lasts a lifetime, will one day begin to believe he saw Claire on the streets a whole day before he actually saw her, presentiment in her wistful shape—or was it Lucy?—foreboding of future weight). Lucy, standing transfixed at the bedroom window, swishes her hand as if gnats were playing at her eyes: Claire adrift in the backyard hammock, with a boy from Ft. Wayne by her, his uniform half covered in chiffon and her hair trailing like water through his hands, both swinging in the sunlight muted by trees. *Oh Claire!* Her laugh a tinkling of crystal.

Lucy doesn't move, Helen in the living room asleep but pulling in her sleep at Lucy's shoulder: wake up! Then Claire, pulling the boy (who would go *any*where) behind her, one hand at her mouth so wide with grinning Lucy can't recognize it, sneaks past Lucy's window; turning at the corner of the house, Claire lifts her head, and waves. Lucy runs to the front door screen to watch them both running down the street. Claire's dress fills with light and, among the folds of light, Lucy sees she wears no underclothes.

Helen's mouth is open in sleep, her head thrown lower than her body and a trickle of saliva running down one side of her face. Lucy's breath catches between these two pictures, as if she won't breathe fully again.

"I better take off work and drive you around," says Lucy at breakfast. "Well," says Helen, and in the afternoon she slouches in the passenger's seat and smokes, saying over and over, "I could just kill him," meaning James. Then she almost sleeps and doesn't watch Lucy edging over to the bad side of town or care when Lucy stops in the "No Parking" spot at the Greyhound Bus station where Claire is slung against the Taxi Only sign. Lucy watches a breeze wrap Claire's skirt around the metal pole before she nudges Helen. "Look."

"Ah ha!" cries Helen, and she doesn't pay attention to where they are but throws herself from the car as Lucy buries her head, arms wrapped across the steering wheel as she listens to Helen's shoes, then, "I've *got* you!"

Claire begins screaming.

Helen is so big they said when she was pregnant no one noticed. So Claire hasn't a chance; Lucy unlocks the back door and Helen pushes her in. "Hush! I can't think!" says Helen, over and over. Lucy doesn't look back but drives with her head forward because they are fighting. "Make her *hush*," cries Helen, but Lucy is driving.

It was because Claire wouldn't hush that the Doctor got her. Lucy would write him that piece of news after she moved away. She will say, "My mother kept telling me to stop anywhere, so I did. She said her ear drums were about to bust. I didn't know you had an office there."

But Helen sees it immediately. "Ha!" So she drags Claire in and, as the door opens, Lucy takes one quick look and sees the waiting room is empty and that Helen is pushing Claire toward a light in the back. Then the door closes. The car is so quiet!

Helen comes out alone, she tells Lucy to take her home, she lies on the sofa, staring upward until the clock on the piano has let one hour pass. Lucy sits on the piano bench with her hands between her knees as she watches Helen. Then Helen fixes her hair, smoothes her hose, and goes for Claire alone. From the bench, Lucy sees that she walks to the car tilted forward and, if it were raining, the pads of her feet would make marks on the ground. Lucy rises to make Claire's bed.

After that, no one except Lucy knew quite what happened, which, perhaps, is why Lucy began her correspondence, the Doctor a purlieu although now she would have nothing to say, childhood, *if* one gets to the other side, an intermediate point beyond which words are useless. *Time getting used up*, Lucy would write to him in her last letter, signing off as if he were a lover used and wasted.

"He *touched* me," says Claire, giggling. "All over, you know?" she asks Helen, tilting her head, plopping one finger in her red mouth, curling on the spead of her beg and giggling.

It doesn't stop.

Helen goes to the bedroom door to watch and when Claire finally falls asleep, Helen closes the door and says, "I wish she'd a screamed."

And Claire wakes up giggling: *he touched me.*

"Why," says Helen, rising from her bowl of cereal, "I almost *believe* her," which is, by afternoon, beside the point; in fact, it will take weeks before Helen can find time to concentrate on that question, because now Claire's laughing is like a dog whistle and Helen is sure *she* will go mad.

Helen or Claire—it hardly matters. "I'm laying myself off, *for* the time being," Lucy tells the manager of the hotel, who says sweetly she knows best, compassion an invitation—over Claire's laughing, one of the last true things Lucy ever tells Claire is that *she'd* take a boy from Ft. Wayne *any* day. Claire nods. Touches her belly. "He did!" she says. "All over."

And Helen, because she has read articles in *Reader's Digest,* takes Claire off to the hospital for, as they say, "observation." "Just for observation," she tells James on the phone, and he says can't you do anything right?

"Honest," says Helen to Lucy as she hangs up the phone—a single word and Lucy is bone-cold.

"She better get herself out of there," Helen says. "She better shape up." And by the hospital piano, Lucy tells Claire. Claire eats everything visitors bring the other patients—chocolate and cookies and doughnuts beside her on the piano bench as she plays over and over "Bringing in the Sheaves." Claire won't speak; on the ward, an old woman says to Lucy, "But everybody loves her."

Then Claire is fat.

She gets out just in time to see Lucy graduate, afterwhich Lucy gets married so quickly all the relatives say she didn't even take time to change her dress, "as if she thought she's go crazy too," in white.

And that is what Lucy thought.

After they got Claire installed in a secretary's job in Atlanta, Lucy said to Helen, "I just can't help you any more."

"Help! Help?" says Helen, on the phone now, trying to find out *how* to find out if the Doctor really did touch Claire.

Before leaving town, Lucy takes herself to his office to stand before him for no more than two minutes, to look. "I just wanted to see," she says, and he smiles as well as he can—his business declining, his wife turning silent. Then Lucy goes away.

As if to bolster herself, Lucy has a child before she writes to him. The letters are a secret because what she wants to say amazes her: "I thought I'd tell you (voice of a child) I think you did it and I know why and even if you get run out of town I want to tell you I understand, I really do."

And, in time, he did move, not because of Helen or even his patients who made speeches before returning to his examination table ("trust" and "loyalty" and "*we* knew your father") but because he began to feel chilled, as if his stomach were a yolk which wouldn't set without more heat. And they forwarded Lucy's letters there.

Who does she think she *is*, he would say to himself, the word *privacy* the only anodyne he knew as Lucy wrote: "I keep thinking in my mind what she said when you said, 'What seems to be the matter,' and what she said was—quiet, like she can be—'I'm pretending, that's what,' so all I mean to say is you understood and then it happened, I mean that's what I think because it works that way sometimes if it gets very quiet."

He never wrote himself, why write? because she said, "I don't know how to tell you except to say they don't remember but we learned to pay attention and that's what's wrong because it's almost like being sick, only you aren't, you know?"

Then Lucy grew up and, sending the picture of her child, apologized for having bothered him.

Some days, walking home, he would see a woman like Claire; he would want her to begin screaming, as if she would return to a former shape followed by music, if the voice turned inside out because, heat or no heat, Lucy was everywhere. And, of course, Lucy would not come to be where he was. No need, eyes everywhere jumping, regardless of weight.

Lucy, he would say, if he could, *I am so very tired*,

and she would say, *You're pretending!*

and they would laugh—children.

Obbligato

The story my father tells me is like the music one wants to make oneself, or hears inside oneself and nowhere else, elusive, as anything which is always present.

He is here, seated on a rattan chair over which he has spread a sheet so that the rough, woven reeds won't snag his suit, a navy pinstripe, the shirt blue, and the tie a maroon wool. It is the kind of picture which stays: like dreams, he turns up at intervals which have no pattern the mind knows. I imagine his spreading the sheet over any chair, in any room he drops himself into. It would be, if not the imperfections of rattan, cat hairs, falling hair, dandruff, nail parings, the sloughing of the skin itself.

"Well, Honey," he says, the chest expanding with air as he smiles. By which he takes me into the time of his real life. Scoops me up. *His* time, though the teeth are white as ever, all there. When he dies, I will put over his grave the smallest, most beautiful wooden cross, and its shadow like a knife will draw his children out.

"Nice place," he says, looking around the room which has mostly space to make it noteworthy. He likes space.

"Well," I answer, a statement; and he sees, because I always settle in—slow movement of absorption—there is nothing to do with me but to have me dress well (he inspects) and take me to dinner. Otherwise . . . . We don't know.

Lavish: we walk together like crowned heads, and the service instantly improves. The chef would come out from behind his stove, but he is not dressed for it, has not worn in years the appropriate white hat.

Wine, candles, and "You look very pretty. A bit thin," he adds. "I always liked my women with some meat on them, you know?" He laughs, so fine a laugh people turn. "Are you taking your vitamins?"

And here, amidst the spoons and a sprinkling of parmesan cheese on the table cloth, I want to tell him I live on will. The body opens for it.

He tells me his story over coffee. It is always some story. I couldn't count the stories; I wouldn't have him know one of his girls is listening. He thinks it is his life, happening simply. A man has to keep his head above water. (And *his* father was graceful, too, although the world did not know it, twelve children and his wife broad—imagine, for instance, the Red Sea parting. Were the images ever of women going through in dresses size 46½? *He* had nothing to say about himself. "To survive, count *up*: five holes in the head, a dozen shins, twenty mandible bones. . . ." But I made that up when he died, art of necessity. Everyone I love is coy with himself, and the cold ground is never, afterwards, indifferent.)

And so the story is also a dream.

It is summer and hot as it always is in Georgia, when the air itself is asking for air. His clothes stick and he drives with the shirt cuffs rolled, the suit coat folded on the wool covers of the LaSalle. He doesn't say where he is going, and that is like him, not because he never said, although that is true, but because, on these roads, the sun curdles the tar and the weeds grow right to the road so it is as if one were in a swamp and knows it, the curves in the road little eddies filling it over and over. In such cases, he wouldn't speak of destination, undoing the land and the way we all know the mind rides on it.

The sun moves, but he doesn't have a watch and the sun moves too slowly to tell time by. Everything but the road is brown or a shade of beige like shetland sweaters.

Maybe he is whistling a western song—no radio in the rebuilt car, the hood so far away from where he holds the steering wheel with one hand it is as if someone is driving him. He looks around and sees nothing but the grass and trees stuck behind the rises which stand in for hills. He takes his left shoe off and rests his foot by the air vent. So, then, when he had to stop, it was that left, shoeless foot that he put into action.

"Well, shit," my father says, "I looked and I looked again, may even have looked a *third* time."

As it was, a baby was crawling across the road, his eyes following it from the instant he saw the shape, and the car following his eyes—he was in the wrong lane when he finally stopped. "As if—Christ—I wanted to run it down."

He stirs his coffee, the teaspoon on the cup a bell clapper as he smiled to himself at foolishness, when the eye and the body work together perfectly, the only, I suppose, real crime of passion.

He didn't back up and park the car; he ran, limping on the shoeless foot, and got the baby and put it in the car on the seat by him, on top of the suit coat, although he said later he wondered if he should have done that since the baby was naked—"little white girl, with curls."

She cried while he backed up and thanked his lucky stars no cars had come and hit him from behind. She slipped against the right-hand door handle when he tried to get his car off the road and discovered weeds hid a ditch. Then she howled; he repeated over and over, "Hush, you hush." His teeth were close, as if grinding in sleep.

I didn't ask if he put on his shoe before he got out and began carrying the baby up through the grass. Such detail: an easiness, like that the baby feels as he holds her to him and rubs the spot where she hit the door handle. The baby would go off with anyone.

"I kept walking and didn't see a thing, you know?" He looked off at the brick wall where a matador in plaster of Paris was spearing a bull.

I guessed I did know. "Did she cry again?"

"Nah," he said. "Why should she cry? I had her."

Then—how long did it take?—he saw the house, one of those unpainted clapboard houses which make nice textures in black and white photographs. No underpinnings, chickens in the yard.

"But they weren't chickens," my father says. "I looked a *fourth* time, Honey. They were children."

The baby should cry.

He picked his way through—I saw it that way because he didn't count heads. Then he remembered the language he had traded in long ago for the voice which got him women, and he called, "Anybody to home?"

I ask him, my eyes on his mouth, "Say it again." But he waves his hand and the Camel cigarette leaves a circle of smoke, gesture of modesty. *Anybody to home?*

He looked around him then and he remembered that the sun was setting, how the porch looked reddish and the light moving so fast the rocking chair seemed to move. Or maybe a child had just jumped from it. He went to the screen door and the girl twisted around, trying to open it. He thought then it was very nice of her not to have peed on his pants to his suit, which he had expected because of the jostling he'd put her throught. He decided he liked her. Like that, he went in.

He tells me, "There wasn't a sound in the house but someone beating on a pan. The kids outside had noticed me going in, so a few of them came up on the porch and looked in. I heard them pressing on the screen behind me— maybe they even ripped it a little. So I stood there—two rooms and a little back room added on—you know, when someone thinks he's going to modernize the place and put in a toilet. Never does," he adds, his history behind him like a crescent moon. "Everything looked a little red, because of the sun. Baby didn't make a sound, as if she knew I wanted her quiet. Guess I did," he says, and he laughs.

"I inched up to the door of the little side room and peeked around. I saw the baby first, banging on a saucepan with a wooden spoon. Must have been the one she had after the one I was holding. It was tiny, had on a little orange-colored diaper. A girl. I think they were all girls. Wouldn't you know?" He rolls her eyes.

I ask what about her.

He says, "'Her?' Oh, you mean the mother. Well, sure, Honey, she was on the bed. Looked like your mother. Of course I haven't seen your mother in quite some time, but she looked like she did as I remember her. Pretty. She looked up at me, didn't move otherwise. She had on a slip, beige, with white lace, and her skin was that white too. I remember.

"So, shit, I looked at her."

I think she must have turned her head away. The baby on the floor beat on the pan and the one he held did not cry—a kind of quiet, like praying when it's useless. The wish drops into a well of disbelief. You learn early not to do it and then, later, the body remembers of its own accord: pure energy dead-set against death, after which what presumes to be real begins receding. It must have been a quiet like that.

He finally asked her (or asked the prone body and the closed eyes where the lashes fluttered), "This yours?" Meaning the baby, because this is his story and he means what he says with a precision which includes all objects breathing or latent. His voice is a hymnal and you just sing along.

My father clears his throat. "Think we need some pistachio ice cream?" he asks me. I don't think we do. "Well," he says, tired, "that's about all. I did get her to look back up. She said, 'Sure, whose did you think she was,' and I said, 'Well, she was in the road,' and she said, 'So put her down.' I did, right where I was. She crawled over to the other one and started beating on the pan. Didn't miss a beat.

"So then the mother turned over on her side, facing the window and that was that. I guessed I looked at her a while, I mean, why not? There she was."

As he walked out, the children at the screen ran off. I imagined they were under the house and the steps, and, maybe, they followed him silently to the first rise. If they had been boys, they would have followed him all the way, sneaking in the grass, and watching him work at getting the car out of the ditch.

But he did that alone, the only sign of him after he drove off and the red dust settled, the rut where the right tires had made an impression. There was no wind. And it was darker now.

Did he stop early to sleep or did he drive on longer than usual?

My father looks up and says, "Funny."

Turning over the check and slapping his hip pocket, he seems weary, or it is me. He tips too much and on the way to my house sings a Stephen Foster song such as my mother sang, and he doesn't realize he's singing.

My mother is more tired than any of us. One day she put down her sheet music, and her rib cage, expanded from years of proper breathing, sank closer to the internal organs. It gave her a shape we couldn't locate because she looked younger and yet we were almost sure that wasn't it. In every photograph, she is shown before one house or another, as if she had just come outside to wait, which is not a misrepresentation. To ask her questions, her daughters had to visit her there, in twilight, under a tree where she unfolded the canvas chair. Crickets made a sound so relentless it seemed she was right to be waiting.

Her eyes as shown in my pictures grew larger over the years, whole notes holding. Her theory belonged to the old school—keeping the timing the composer intended. But in the house, she squinted, and over her ribs she grew a layer of fat. Not pretty in years, but her eyes hold a memory of beauty, and they make me ache. I look and look away, keeping on purpose my body small.

That night my father grinds his teeth in sleep; and if a person has done this once, he knows the rhythm keeps the body beached and heaving, the vortex imagined and inaccessible. I want to break into the sound of water and go, then, into my son's room, to look at him.

Yet there is no need to mention him, except to say *one* and *boy* and that, standing in his room where night lights filtered through plaid curtains, I know he is not like the rest of us. Anyone could love him; he is not infected.

Even when he stands perfectly still and smells the voluble air, he thinks the world is fine, and what is not is a joke. I would *never* scoop him up. And when his father, in remorse, tried to, I left him. So simple, like my father's language, when, long after the fact, I knew what I had done.

There lies my gracefulness, sleeping.

By dawn, my father is sick, a mundane heaving, and what I hear first is his cursing. I think it is his cure. I want him on his way and lie awake as if it were *my* valise sitting packed by the door, and everything down the road to be passed by.

But in the morning, he is hot, his teeth drawn over his lips, and the swearing bitter. Who *is* this, washing up over the coverlet salt as if it contain air: "God-damn-son-of-a-bitch-Jesus-H.-Christ I *hate* it."

He named all his daughters with such care they bear their names in the way their wrists move, as others have worn the blue tatoo. What *is* his living? *They* refuse to hear his stories.

Once, during the four days he stays wrapped in covers and this language like gauze, he comes into the living room with his hair matted, the blue pajamas soaked, and says from the doorway, "Damn it, if you have to go on studying and studying"—his right arm sweeping to take in all the books— "at least for Christ's sake keep it *out* of the bedroom when they take you *in*."

Tell me a story.

Even, with a paring knife, I curl the strips of carrots I bring him on a plate. I think: in dreams he will grow feet and on his feet, tires, and under his body a car will bloom like black orchids, and he will get to Santa Fe or the outskirts of Tuscon or Maitland, Florida by dusk.

Then he is well and sounds like himself: "Honey, fix me up a lunch to take along." And so I fix him a picnic basket full of fine food, and, tucked inside, the Methodist hymnal my mother gave me. I put it by the red gingham napkin, by which I meant I loved him.

He calls from the car, "See you when I see you. Send an address if you move," and I wave and wave as the car moves out of sight.

In the quiet of my familiar self, I clean the house and when I pass by a mirror, I see that I am smiling.

Later, when it is dark and I know he has been through twilight on the road and I hear outside the crickets rubbing their legs together, I stop, a dream pulling my eyelids down. It almost goes away. I see my father crawling into a service station on his last ounce of gas. The attendant says, "Just made it," and he says, "Why sure."

But that is not the image, no.

No: at twilight, he drove through Georgia and, looking a third time, he sees me, a shape, crawling across the road. He is tired now and both shoes are on because it is cooler, and the car barely swerves as it follows his eyes, as if he knew this were coming. Which knowing cannot be.

But he picks me up and, slowly, carries me to the house. He goes right in and, there, all the children are gathered. So he hands me to the oldest one, who wedges me between her legs and continues singing.

He takes a quick look into the side room where she is as she was, uncovered, though it is cooler even in the house, and he says, "In the road again." Her back is turned and he stays to look at her, the boat-shape her body makes from the shoulder to the toes, until he raises one eyebrow, shrugs, and goes.

It is so late the tire tracks are invisible. A wind is blowing.

And the next day, driving through Georgia . . .

Except, from now on, my sisters, receiving me over and over, roll their eyes. And my mother, turning, looks. And he looks away.

She should have been better at the improvised song; she might have ridden on the right-hand side. Long or short trip, at least *her* head would have rested higher than the handle.

And he, though he *never* intended, has me listening: "Hush, you hush."

To which I say in recompense: in my bed the eye and the body work together perfectly. The perfect crime, the refined amulet, of passion.

Printed January 1979 in Santa Barbara
& Ann Arbor for the Black Sparrow Press
by Mackintosh and Young & Edwards Brothers Inc.
Design by Barbara Martin. This edition is
published in paper wrappers; there are
200 hardcover copies numbered & signed by
the author; & 26 copies have been
handbound in boards by Earle Gray & are
lettered & signed by the author.

Eve Shelnutt, who teaches fiction at Western Michigan University in Kalamazoo, Michigan, was born in Spartanburg, South Carolina. She received the B.A. degree from The University of Cincinnati and, in 1973, the M.F.A. from The University of North Carolina at Greensboro, under the auspices of the Randall Jarrell Fellowship. Her first short story won the Mademoiselle Fiction Award and, since then, she has published stories in a number of literary journals, including *Virginia Quarterly Review*, *American Review*, *The Literary Review*, *Northwest Review*, *Mississippi Review*, and *Ohio Review*. One of her stories appeared in the *O. Henry Prize Collection* and was reprinted in the Bantam anthology *Stories of the Modern South*. A critical article about *The Love Child* appeared in the August 1978 issue of *Ploughshares*. In 1977 she was a fellow at the Virginia Center for the Creative Arts at Sweetbriar. *The Love Child* is her first published book.